This is something I made. I am going to sell it to pay bills, enjoy life, and donate to charity. But I won't try to wring every last dollar out of it. As such, the copyright for this work will become more permissive over time and eventually it will be in the public domain—48 years sooner than is typical. I don't have lawyers to try and stop you, but for the first 10 years of publication, please don't steal this book and try to make money off it.

Buy lots of copies for friends and for your local library.

The copyright for this book expires December 31, 2048. After this date, the author considers it to be in the Public Domain. Because 70 years is too long. Please see the URL at the bottom of this page for the latest permissions.

This book is a memoir and reflects the author's recollections of experiences over time. Some names and characteristics have been changed, some events have been conflated, and some dialogue has been recreated. This book is a work of fiction. Some names, characters, and incidents portrayed in it are the work of the author's imagination. Any resemblance to actual persons—living or dead—events, or locations is entirely coincidental.

A thing can be two things.

Do me a favor: take good care of yourself today.

~Matthew.

Copyright © 2023 by Matthew Oliphant

First edition October 2023

ISBN 979-8-9868545-2-6 (paperback)

ISBN 979-8-9868545-3-3 (ebook)

Library of Congress Control Number: 2022918807

matthewoliphant.com/iso

IN SEARCH OF

a faulty memoir of things that probably never happened

I hope you like the book you are about to read even if it isn't this one.

DEDICATION

It's just Claire.

DEDICATION

ANCHORAGE

A way of seeing is also a way of not seeing.

—Kenneth Burke

I arrive at Club Paris precisely six minutes prior to the start of my shift. It is my second job, but it is only part-time, so I am not here that often. When it is my day to come in, I make sure to come early as Armon plates something for me to eat. For free.

I sit at the table in the back where Stan usually sits. It is a terrible table for guests as it is directly across from the entry to the kitchen. Even when this place is extremely busy on a Saturday night, they will not sit anyone at this table. No one wants to hear "Corner," being yelled through their dinner as servers and bussers—which is me—go in and out of the kitchen trying to not collide with each other.

Within a few bites of a giant pile of excellent mashed potatoes, Stan slides into the booth across the table from me. He is one of the owners, or the son of one of the owners. I am not sure which. Probably both. *Club Paris* has been around since the fifties and I think it has been in Stan's family the whole time.

Fancy meeting you here, I say.

Stan chuckles and says, "Don't you have work to do?"

Not for another forty-three seconds, I say, shoveling more mash into my mouth.

I saw Stan a few hours ago at the Downtown location for *Cafe del Mundo*. He came in while I was there so that he could use my employee discount to get a *Gaggia* home espresso machine. I get free coffee while working there, so I do not need a machine at home and I figure someone should benefit from my discount.

"Thanks again for the hook up," says Stan as he lays out a few piles of receipts to start going over the books.

Yeah, of course, I say.

Forty-three seconds being up, I excuse myself, bus my dishes—as I am now on the clock—put on my apron, and hop to it. With as much hop as I can muster given I have been up since five this morning. Most of my shift is spent clearing tables, seating people now and again, and being chastised for not knowing to place the brandy snifters directly on the cups of coffee by ego-driven white men who think ties are important. Fucking yuppies.

The front of *Club Paris* is lined with large windows that look out onto 5th Avenue. As I clear one of the tables at the window, I can see the light from the setting sun landing on the mall across the street, but the light looks much dimmer than it should given the time of day and that the weather forecast is for clear skies.

I lean against the window and look west to see the sky turning black. I set down the tray stacked with partially-filled water glasses and napkins and step outside to look at what is happening. Stan follows me. He likely watched me walk out, wondered why I was leaving mid-shift, and followed me out. I can tell he is about to ask what I am up to, but then looks where I am looking. The sky is definitely turning black.

There is still a sliver of sun above *Sleeping Lady*, but it looks dull brown instead of bright orange-yellow. From the ground to as high as I can see, there is a wall of black clouds heading toward us. Not even clouds really. One solid mass of black.

I walk to the corner of 5th and E streets. I look north, toward my daytime job at *del Mundo* and can see blue sky. I look south. More blue sky. Though, in both directions, the light is looking more and more washed out.

I walk back to stand next to Stan and tell him what I saw.

"Weird weather," he says, with a bit of a questioning uplift to his voice.

I suppose, I say.

We walk back inside together and get back to work. I finish clearing the table by the window and take the dishes back to the dishwasher. I am glad I do not have the job of dishwasher. It looks like very uncomfortable work. And yet, it is the second most important job in the place behind the *Chef de Cuisine*—aka Armon. I suspect though that Juan is not paid as well as Armon.

I head back to the floor and begin filling water glasses at tables around the room. I look out the window again and the light filtering in looks... weird. I head up to the front again and peek out the window. My eyes widen and I walk out the front door again, still holding the water pitcher.

The sky is still mostly blue behind me to the east, but somewhere down by K Street the buildings are being engulfed by the black. I estimate only ten minutes have passed since Stan and I stood out here.

At a steady pace, like water pouring into a dry gulch, the blackness comes straight at me.

I look to the east again. The sky is clear, but it is definitely getting darker than it should be at this time of day. By the time I turn back around, the buildings at H Street are being engulfed. Cars along 5th Avenue have come to a stop. A few people are standing next to their car, looking down the street, and wondering the same thing I am wondering in this moment: what in the fuck is happening?

I cannot make out any buildings west of F Street now—they are gone.

"Hey. Come back inside."

I turn to see Stan in the doorway, looking west with me. He is not at all perturbed that I am out here when I should be working. The tone in his voice is definitely about my safety. I walk back in, letting him hold the door open for me. I set the water pitcher on the host stand and look back at the window. Most of the people here for an early dinner are standing at the window looking out.

Stan claps his hands a few times, loudly, to get everyone's attention.

"Folks. I don't know what's going on, but we're going to ask that everyone stay inside for a bit."

The small crowd murmurs their way back to their tables except for an older couple who remain standing by the window. They are holding hands and leaning so the sides of their heads touch. She has long, gray hair and stands about an inch taller than him. He has a buzzed haircut which makes it difficult to make out the color, but it is probably gray, too. They look very comfortable together. And familiar, too, but I cannot place from where.

My attention is drawn from them back outside. From the right side of the window, the view fills in with darkness. It is still bright on the left side of the window, but within moments, the darkness pushes the light out of the way. As the entire window is filled, the darkness changes to a medium gray and the streetlights wink on.

It is snowing. In summer. It is Alaska, but it does not snow during the summer in Anchorage.

The snow is gray and it covers everything. Within minutes there is an inch of snow on top of the mail and newspaper boxes across the street. The streetlights are barely casting enough light to see. The entire restaurant is staring out the window in complete silence except for the couple at the window.

"It is pretty in a way, like you said," says the woman.

"Indeed. Just as I remembered," says the man.

He stands back from the window and gestures that they should leave with her leading the way. They walk out together into the gray snowscape, with Stan encouraging them to stay inside.

Anika, who works the bar, uncovers the television that hangs on the wall. *Club Paris* is not the kind of place that has a TV running all the time, but when the Super Bowl or similar sporting event is on, it is a big draw. She powers it up and turns the knob to Channel 2.

My close, personal friend—as I like to call her—Jackie Purcell stands in front of a weather graphic on the green screen behind her and a picture of a mountain in the upper right-hand corner of the screen. Underneath the picture reads: MT REDOUBT ERUPTS.

I assume it is in allcaps due to the fact that a volcano is erupting and spreading ash all over Alaska's most populated city. Maria Downey cuts in to Jackie's weather report to inform viewers that KLM Flight 867 has just recovered from a two mile drop and will be doing an emergency landing at ANC. The ash and debris from the eruption took out all four engines.

A two mile drop.

"Okay. Just a volcano. Not end of times. Buss some tables."

Stan smiles as he says it, but the look on his face is a mix of tension and relief. I shrug and get back to it. By the time my shift is over, and tips are split, the fact that it is still raining ash outside is not that big of an issue.

Except for the fact that the only way for me to get home is to drive. And cars use air to move. Air that is filled with fine ash.

I spend twenty minutes waffling on what to do. Stan gives me the classic, "you don't have to go home, but you can't stay here," and I decide to go for it. I leave through the back door as my car is parked against the wall in the alley behind the restaurant. I am relieved that I had the forethought to wet a towel and tie it around my nose and mouth. Even with this precaution, I can taste ash in my mouth.

I get in, close the door as quickly as possible, then close the vents. The 164 has a handle that opens a flap which allows air to rush in from the foot well. Very advanced design, Volvo. Kudos. I make sure that the vent is well shut and start up the car. It sounds completely normal, so I flip on the wipers, put it in reverse and back out, narrowly avoiding Stan's motorcycle. I do not envy his ride home.

I maneuver between boxes, dumpsters, and other cars that fill up the alley and make my way to 4th, then C Street, then 6th for the drive home. As I pass *Merrill Field*—noting that no planes are flying at the busiest small plane airport in the world—I get a sense that the car is having its first issue. When I lift my foot from the accelerator, then depress it again, the engine does not respond as immediately as it typically does.

By the time I pull into the driveway at home, I can hear a persistent, low-toned grinding sound. I put it in park, turn off the lights, and turn off the engine. It shudders to a stop. Out of curiosity, I try turning it over again. It grinds and shakes, then dies.

I love Sasha—the name of my car—but I think I just killed her.

Volvo, non volvunt.

"**You're** in a rut," Meg says to me, as I put a freshly-made latte in front of her. She sits at the counter next to the espresso machine when the other two of The Lesbians Three are not around. Mostly to bother me, I suspect, though in truth, I welcome it.

A what, I ask.

Steam hisses out of the frothing nozzle as I clear it of milk.

"Volcanoes notwithstanding, you're in a rut. I can see it. Same thing every day. You come in, make coffee, go home."

True, though I sometimes find myself dining out or attending the theater, I say.

I pronounce it *tay-ah-truh* because I am fancy.

Meg laughs. "Seriously. You need to get out of here."

The cafe?

"No. Alaska. Just get the fuck out of here. I don't care where you go, but it's time to make a move."

To the casual observer, in this case, Ian, sitting two stools over from Meg, this conversation may seem a little aggressive, but Meg pokes at me a lot like this. She knows me and knows what is best for me, so she says. She often has a lot of life advice for me which I rarely agree with, but this time I find myself nodding in response, as I pull the eleventy-thousandth shot of the day, thinking that she is likely onto something.

I notice Natalie and Joan walk in, without ordering, and take a seat at their usual Holding Court table. As I take the drink I made to the customer waiting at the register, I get a nod from Joan, which I assume means to bring them their usual. In my cafe—not that it is, but I pretend it to be—royalty does not have to wait in line.

Of the people who come to Midtown *del Mundo*, Natalie, Joan, and Meg are the ones I gravitate toward. They let me sit with them and often regale me with stories from their past—Natalie, with great stories about growing up in *Nantes* and Joan, if she is to be believed, with stories about growing up in *Tilikaklit, Alaska.*

I wander back to the espresso machine to make their drinks ahead of the current build-up of orders. Meg wanders away from the counter to join Natalie and Joan with a "Think about it..." said over her shoulder.

"Looks like I miss a lot of good haranguing," says Ian.

You do, but life is better at Downtown. I don't like it here in Midtown, I say.

I am stuck in the Midtown location because I am in trouble with the actual owner of *del Mundo* for using my employee discount for Stan. I am not sure why I am still employed—especially given his anger about it—but mostly I am unsure why it is a big deal at all. But, here I find myself, making drinks for Absolutely No Caffeine Woman, lawyers with fancy cars, insurance agents with NFL sons, and the one and only bright spot being their royal highnesses, The Lesbians Three.

"Such wind as scatters young men through the world, to seek their fortunes farther than at home, where small experience grows," proclaims

Ian.

He works for the Anchorage Opera and I assume his words are from a currently running show.

What, I ask.

"Shakespeare," he says. "Which explains why the quote says men and not people."

I nod. I ask him to repeat the quote and he does.

"The second best thing about scattering yourself through the world is eventually you get to come back," he adds.

What is the first best thing, I ask.

"That's for you to find out," says Ian with a wink. "Gimme another Sawdust muffin."

I laugh and walk to the middle of the long counter to grab a bran muffin from the pastry tray. I put a napkin on a small plate and gently rest the muffin on it. I return to Ian, lower my head, and present it to him saying, Honored Lord.

It gets him to laugh, which is the point. He pulls the muffin apart into two roughly equal pieces and dunks one piece into his coffee. He lets it rest there, soaking up the coffee.

"Let me put it to you like this," he says. "If you stay in one place long enough you're bound to see someone you know pass by. Double the chance if you stay in your hometown. Double that again if its a small hometown. Double that again if it's a small, hometown graveyard."

He puts the coffee-imbued muffin in his mouth, a pleased-with-himself smile on his face as he chews.

I feel like I can shorten that to a simple go-on-git, I say in response.

He picks up the other half of the muffin and begins the dunking sequence.

"Not everything has to be seen through the lens of efficiency," he says, his smile abruptly leaving his face.

He does not look offended, but I do not quite take his meaning. I hear a "hey" next to me and notice the line of customers is quite long. I nod to Angela who is giving me a *help-me* look. I leave Ian to his sawdust and jump back on the line.

The next few hours fly by. I spend most of my time on the machine and even have my lunch interrupted by two regular customers who plead with me to make their drinks. "No one makes it like you," one of them says, which appeases my ego.

I go back inside to make their drinks, cutting my lunch short by twenty minutes. I reclaim that time at the end of my shift, letting everyone know that I am taking advantage of the afternoon lull, and walk back to the office to get my things. Perry, the owner, is rummaging through a pile of receipts and does not acknowledge me at all.

I hang my special apron on its hook—an apron without a neck strap as those give me migraines. I grab my keys and give Perry one last opportunity to at least say hello. He does not. I grab the handle of the door, turn it, and surprise myself by interrupting him.

You know, I say, this place really needs a good cleaning.

He looks up with a mild glare.

Like, a really deep clean, I say. I leave the thought lingering.

"And," he asks.

I think you should let me put together a group of volunteers to deep clean the place some night after close, I explain. Pay everyone normal wages, buy them pizza, and play loud music.

"Yeah," he says, drawing out the word.

Think about it, I say. This place has been open for, what, well over a decade. It is cleaned every day, but, have you ever been up on the counter and looked behind the coffee bins, I ask.

The bins are all shiny brass with glass fronts to see the beans and a handle that twists to allow gravity to pour the beans through a chute and into whatever container is needed at the time. Earlier in the day, I climbed onto the counter to dust some of the plants. This allowed me to see behind the wall of bins. We fill the bins by lifting the lid on the top, then dumping in the beans—all of which is well above head-height for all who work here.

I bet we could put together several pounds of coffee from what is back there, I say.

That gets him on board. I doubt he has looked behind those bins since he put them in.

"Yeah, okay. Not a bad idea," he says, giving me the first positive emotion in a few weeks.

Cool, I say. I'll find a few people and we can pick a date.

"Okay," he says, and turns back to the pile of papers in front of him.

Things have been very tense between us since he moved me from Downtown to Midtown. I suppose offering this up is a way to attempt to mend things. Also, I am incredibly curious to brew some espresso with ten-year-old beans. It will be gross, but also amazing.

I open the door and close it gently behind me. I walk behind the counter, grab my tips, and head toward the door.

"Rut" I hear shouted from the direction of the Holding Court table. Their

Highnesses, praise be their names, have apparently returned for afternoon tea. I brush it off and drive home in a car I am borrowing which is not pervaded with volcanic ash. No one is there, as usual.

It is still the middle of the afternoon, but I decide to go upstairs and lay down on my bed. I think about the day. About the preening Midtown customers, sawdust muffins, and ruts. Meg might be onto something.

The persistent late-summer sun floods through the windows—the wind is taking the ash to the west now—making the room so very bright, but I am asleep within minutes.

I dream.

"**I** have the other half of a round-trip ticket you can use," offers Molly.

We sit at the special corner table, the only table with some privacy, in *Sacks* and I am enjoying a *Yuppie Special*—it is my favorite and I enjoy ordering it in the back-of-house vernacular the staff use.

Really, I ask, feeling a bit incredulous.

"Yeah, I'm not leaving Alaska for a while and I don't really need a one-way ticket to Seattle."

I ponder this as I have another bite of the chicken breast with gorgonzola sauce. It is so tangy and good that my eyes roll back into my head and I forget for a moment what we are talking about.

How much, I ask, coming back to my senses.

"The change fee and you buy lunch."

Deal, I say, as I take another bite.

Molly covering the fee, plus the fifty for this moderately fancy lunch at a moderately fancy restaurant, means I buy a plane ticket for about half what a round-trip would cost, which I suppose seems reasonable. It is my birthday after all, why not buy a gift for myself? And in that moment, I wonder why I have to pay for lunch on my birthday.

We finish up and drive to *Earthquake Park* to watch the water for a bit. We do not talk much during the drive out and even less while we sit on the trunk of the car I am borrowing. Molly and I spend a lot of time together and most of that time is spent in silence. She is a comfortable and comforting friend and we find ourselves doing activities like this a lot.

The *Cook Inlet* water rolls gently in and out. Somewhere, underneath the tame surf, are bits of houses, people's lives, and likely people's bodies. Several hundred people lived here not too long ago and thanks to a terribly frightening night, it is now a nature park with a scenic viewpoint—which seems like a very human reaction to devastation.

"I got a new film if you want to come over to watch it," says Molly.

Her offer interrupts the silence between us and jolts me out of my reverie on the Quake.

Sure, though I told Natasha I would hang out with her tonight, I say.

"She's welcome to join."

We get back in the car and drive to pick up Natasha from her dorm. She lives on the *Alaska Pacific University* campus and, as far as Anchorage driving goes, it is essentially on the way to Molly's house. We drive into the loop that goes around the large fountain which sits in the middle of the dorm buildings. After so many years of attending art camps on this campus as a kid and two years of going to university here, walking up to the dorms feels like coming home—more so than actual home.

We wander through the common area of the north building. Floor-to-ceiling it takes up three stories. There is a railing on each story above, behind which are the dorm rooms. Someone I recognize vaguely is serenading a small group of people on the floor above with a valiant, if strained attempt at *Danny Boy*.

We find Natasha in her room on the main floor. Her door is open as most doors here tend to be, even into the late hours of the night. I introduce her to Molly and let Natasha know about the movie invite. We did not have specific plans, so with a shrug of *why not* from Natasha, the three of us drive to Molly's place which she shares with her brother, who is away for the summer on a commercial fishing boat.

After a few minutes of gathering snacks and drinks, we settle onto the couch to watch the film. It is called *Henry & June* and is just out on VHS. I know nothing about it and, as the film progresses, I reach for the box to look at the rating: NC-17. I am definitely older than 17, but cannot say I am ready to watch a film like this. Especially with two women, both of whom I am not sleeping with. During the scene where Hugo finds Anaïs and essentially rapes her, which then becomes consensual, we all glance at each other for the first time since the start of the film.

Molly and my eyes linger a bit and an unbidden thought wafts through my brain as to why she is not my girlfriend, given how much time we spend together. My brain provides the obvious answer that we simply do not think of each other in that way. But I find it strange that the thought comes to me at all.

As the awkward eye contact abates, and we continue watching the film, I realize I have not thought about the plane ticket since lunch. I am avoiding it. I do not want to think about leaving. It is possible that I like my coffee-making, gorgonzola-chicken-eating, trunk-sitting, quake-pondering, awkward-sexual-tension-eye-contact rut a bit too much. I roll those likely hyphenated adjectives around my brain and think about how bad that sounds.

Okay, Meg, I get it, I say quietly to myself.

Molly and Natasha both ask "What" in unison, but I shake my head and stay silent. We watch most of the rest of the movie, but turn it off with roughly ten minutes remaining on the tape. We are all tired. Molly invites both me and Natasha to stay the night, but Natasha wants to sleep in her own bed.

We say good night, and I drive south on Lake Otis, turn on Providence, and drive until the road essentially dead-ends at the APU dorms. Natasha gives me a leaning hug, made slightly awkward in that she still wears her seat belt, then gets out and walks up the large, wide staircase to the dorms.

I drive home and as I walk in, I look at the clock on the wall. It is two in the morning and, as usual, I find myself at home, alone.

"COME with me to the Talkeetna Bluegrass Festival," says Natasha.

I do not like bluegrass, I tell her.

"Right, but the point you're missing is that you have a car, I don't, and I want to go," she explains.

So, naturally, I agree to go. Natasha offers to pay for my entry as well as a spot in her tent. My eyebrows go up at that. She notices.

"Not like that," she adds quickly.

Natasha is one of the many people on whom I have a small, non-serious crush. If she ever says, "Hey, let's be a couple," I would shrug and accept it, much like my shrug and acceptance for driving her two hours north for music I do not like. I feel no push to be with her, but I do like being around her.

Frances, another of the non-serious crush people, sets an americano in front of me with a *here-you-go* smile. A small group of us sits together at the *Kaladi* on Brayton. Since being relegated to Midtown *del Mundo*, I spend most of my hanging-out-at-a-cafe time at *Kaladi Brothers*. It is the other big coffee company in Anchorage, and is far more hip, atmosphere-wise. Especially compared to the stuffiness of Midtown. It also helps to have gorgeous friends like Frances who work here and give me free coffee.

Natasha sits next to me, looking happy that I will take her to Talkeetna. Frank sits across from us. He pulls one of the postcards that decorate all the tables from underneath the Plexiglas cover to see who sent it.

Without looking up he asks, "Can I go?"

Please say no, I think loudly.

"Sure," exclaims Natasha.

A few days later, the three of us drive north on AK-1.

We stretch the two-hour trip to three-and-a-half hours with a long stop in Palmer for lunch at *Vagabond*. I like their soups and the big, thick slices of bread that go with.

I am the driver and we will have lunch at Vagabond and Frank will buy, I exclaim to the car, prior to the old-way turnoff.

And it is so.

After a very delicious lunch, we hit the road and arrive at Talkeetna in the early afternoon. It is a typical August day in the Interior: hot. The mosquitoes are waning, but still abundant in this forest of birch and spruce.

We drive past the main entrance and make our way, thanks to the many volunteers in orange vests, along one of the many dirt tracks pretending to be a road. There are a lot of people here already. Hundreds of cars line the dirt track on the left side. I find a spot where I can fit the car into some semblance of a parallel parking job. The spot barely allows enough room to park, and is made more difficult thanks to the ditch I have drive into then straddle to keep the car off the track, but also not actually in the woods.

We find a spot to set up Natasha's tent not too far from the car and, thankfully, not too close to other campers in the woods nearby. The ground cover between the trees is low and easy to traverse. Natasha sets up her tent. I take my bicycle off the rack on the back of the car, wheel it over to the tent, and lean it against a birch tree. I notice Natasha's tent is a two-person tent. I remind her that there are three people in our party as Frank plunks down his backpack next to us.

"Oh, I figure we can swap out and each spend a night in the car," she says.

While I enjoy being spontaneous—sparingly—I do not enjoy sleeping in cars. The festival is three days long and, to get it out of the way, I volunteer to be in the car the first night.

Beyond purchasing our tickets, we do not spend any time at the festival the first night. Dinner is at *Kahiltna Bistro*. Again, I let Natasha and Frank know that I, as the driver and the first-night-car-sleeper, will not pay. They both have decent paying jobs. Natasha works at the university. Frank works for the state and spends the wee hours of the night-into-morning telling road crews, "You're doing it wrong," for $19 an hour. He does not have to tell them how to do it right, that is someone else's job. Nice work if you can get it.

As we return to the campsite after dinner, the sun is almost completely down. Natasha suggests a campfire.

"I saw they have firewood for sale down at the festival site," she says.

I will get it, I say, striking my best approximation of a Mountain Man pose.

"Why are you standing like that," asks Natasha, laughing.

Mountain Man, I exclaim into the night.

"Uh huh."

I remove my fists from my hips and take my foot off of the tree stump. Obviously she does not know a true Mountain Man when she sees one. Which is likely due to the fact we are not in the mountains and I am not a man.

I take hold of my bike, walk it to the dirt track, and ride it down to the festival area. There is a band playing and a few hundred people fling themselves about in front of the stage, but I ignore it. It is easy enough to find the guy selling firewood. I get a halfhearted reminder about fire safety, then strap ten pieces of firewood to the rack on the back of my bike, tying them down with two bungee cords.

I put the bike in its lowest gear and ride back to the top of the hill. The wood only falls off once, about halfway up the hill. I arrive back at the campsite completely exhausted. This is exactly the kind of use my Cannondale 600 was made for. Probably.

I drop the firewood in front of Natasha and Frank, then walk back to the dirt track to look for rocks to make a ring around the fire. I find some, though not really enough, but it will have to do. We get the fire started quickly and settle in to watch the flames and talk about this and that.

A drive between two and four hours is not all that long in Alaska, but I am tired. I begin to drift as Frank regales us with the purposefully sloppy work tactics of the private companies hired to renew Alaska roads every summer. I bid them good sleep and head to the car.

I sleep terribly. The 1984 Dodge 600 seems oddly ill-suited for this kind of use. Even the Turbo doesn't add much in the way of comfort, though it has saved my life twice before. One would think, as a car designer, that people do sleep in their car from time to time and it might not be such a terrible idea to design for that.

At this time of year, Talkeetna's latitude gets roughly seventeen hours of daylight, so, in addition to the terrible sleeping position, I find it difficult to even rest, let alone sleep. Eventually, the full darkness of night comes to be replaced seemingly immediately by the dawn. I decide it is morning enough and remove the shirt from the window—my haphazard attempt at some privacy from passersby—get out and stretch everything. I glance over at the tent and can tell neither Frank or Natasha are up yet. They are probably, what is that called, oh, right...sleeping.

The early morning air is chilly. I grab my jacket then wander down the dirt track to the festival entrance. No one is guarding it. I walk in, then down the hill's winding path, between the two ruts, to the river.

The large stage is set up at the far end of the clearing. There are stalls set up to sell food and merchandise. Roughly fifty people mill about either setting up stalls, moving things on stage, or trying to figure out when the next band will play even though the music will not start for hours yet—most of those are probably still drunk or stoned.

I walk to the river's edge and kick a rock into the water. I can barely hear the splash as the river makes enough noise to drown it out. I sit on a large rock that is mostly flat across the top. Part of it is in the water, but it is tall enough that I can dangle my legs over the edge with my feet just above the waterline.

Tiny swatches of *Cornus canadensis* line the shore on the other side of the river. The white flowers pop against the green leaves. I lean back with my hands behind me on the rock and stare across the way. A small bird lands in a swatch and flies away with a stick. The chilled breeze coupled with the cold water sets me shivering. My right foot dips into the water a bit and I let it remain there.

At this moment, with the sound of water and the wind drowning out all that is behind me, I am at peace. At this moment, I want to sit at the side of this river forever.

IT is dusk and we can hear music drifting through the forest to our campsite.

We follow the same route as my morning walk, talking about nothing in particular. Natasha buzzes with excitement to be going. Frank and I are here, largely, for something different to do besides hang out in a cafe or watch movies at his place being bothered by his neighbors who seem to think *su casa es su casa*. We can see the bright stage lights from the hill above and, as we descend, the sound of the band and the crowd rises. The number of people milling about, eating food, and dancing seems to grow exponentially as we wind our way closer to the stage. There are a few thousand people crowding the relatively small area by the river. The stage sheds enough sound and light to wash over us all with its energy.

Natasha and Frank wade into the crowd dancing and, much to my surprise, I follow, but cannot last long, deep inside the sea of people, the way Natasha and Frank are able. I tack my way out of the crowd to spend time recovering on my rock by the river, then back again into the flowing mass. Hours pass and even over the loud music my attention is drawn to the sound of wolves. A howl near me, then one far away. More and more voices join in howling. Natasha points and I look up. The sun is no longer there. I did not notice given the lights from the stage, but the sky is bright red with Aurora.

The music quiets a bit as the band clues-in to what is happening above. As if in answer, the red of the Aurora falls away, as do the howls of the thousands of people surrounding me. It feels entirely too quiet, too suddenly. Everyone feels adrift as the Aurora all but vanishes. Then a sudden deep red floods the entire visible sky and the howls respond in kind. The music rushes forward to catch up.

We ebb and flow with the Aurora, trailing off as the red falls away, rising back up as a more intense red washes away the stars. It begins to feel as though we are the ones deciding how the Aurora flows. We howl and the red becomes more brilliant than the stage lights. We run out of air in our lungs and the stars return.

Looking over the crowd, from the stage to where the dirt tracks go back up the hill, our collective movements mirror that of the river beside us. We release energy and it carries away only to fill back up again with each eight-minute-old convulsive release from the sun. An unknowable amount of time passes. It does not matter. Eventually, the Aurora fades completely, indifferent to our cries, and our collective sanity returns.

"What a light show, eh," yells the lead singer of the band.

He yells it loud enough that the speakers *squelch* and the entire crowd exhales a groan of protest at the harsh noise. The band picks up the music again, but the crowd is not interested. Most of the people surrounding us turn their attention away from the stage for their own quiet conversations. I move through them toward the exit, with Frank and Natasha in tow. The murmuring creates its own current. Conversations trickle through my attention and it is clear the collective consciousness of the crowd is trying to hold onto as much of what just occurred as possible.

My senses are awash and, as we make our way back to the campsite, I find that I feel hungry, vulnerable, and yet calm for the first time in a long while—even more than by the river this morning. Or yesterday morning. We are well into the next day by the time we make it back to our camp.

The energy expended over the evening leaves barely enough to clamber over Natasha—who, for some reason is not laying in the spot away from the tent opening—and into my sleeping bag. Frank takes his turn in the car.

I lay back on my improvised jacket pillow and close my eyes. They pop open immediately, as if those few precious moments closed are enough to re-energize me. I shift my hips a bit and realize that I am laying on part of an exposed tree root. I roll to my side and angle my body around it. I am facing Natasha and see that she is facing me.

"That was fun," she says quietly.

Indeed, I say with much satisfaction, even allowing a small smile.

She smiles at me.

"Sleep well," she says, then she rolls over.

I stare blankly at her back then move as much of me off the tree root as possible. I am in as easily an awkward position as my night in the car. My eyes close and I get something akin to the concept of sleep.

When my eyes open, I am alone in the tent. The sun is up and I can hear birds wending their way through the woods. After a few moments teaching my spine to be straight again, I tumble out of the tent to see Frank and Natasha sitting on a log nearby. They both look as though they slept as well as me.

My emergence from the tent interrupts their conversation.

"How did you sleep," asks Frank.

Terribly, but enough, I say.

"Enough to drive," he asks.

He and Natasha catch me up on their conversation, which does not take long as the short-and-short of it is that they are ready to leave. And I am right there with them.

Fine by me, I say, stretching my back side to side. Coffee first, though, I add.

"Coffee first," says Natasha.

"Hot chocolate," says Frank.

Close enough, I say.

We wander down again to the festival area to get energy for the drive.

Between the time we have cups in-hand and make our way back to the campsite, we decide to continue to Fairbanks instead of going back to Anchorage. It is only four and a half hours away, so why not? Frank made tentative plans to meet a few other people there, if he could find a ride from the festival. Natasha and I have nothing better to do so we accompany him.

Five hours later, we meet the other group at the Denny's in beautiful, downtown Fairbanks. I know all of them, though Frank had left it somewhat vague as to who was in the group. Amira, Orla, Lily, Dex, Simon, and Mark. All people with whom I attended high school. All of whom I'm on decent terms with, but rarely ever see. Natasha is the only person in this group with whom I did not go to high school. She only knows me and Frank.

We spend an inordinate amount of time around the biggest table there. We stretch out each order of coffee and fries with gravy, essentially overstaying our welcome, but we keep buying things so they do not kick us out.

Night comes and we determine the best course of action is to all share a hotel room because none of us have enough money for our own rooms and no one in the group thought to make plans ahead of time. Naturally.

Amira and I go to the front desk while the others wait outside, out of view. Apparently, Amira and I are the most respectable-looking.

Good evening, I say, respectably.

"Good evening," says the clerk. "Checking in?"

"Yes. A room for two," says Amira with a little too much emphasis on the number.

"I gotcha," says the clerk with almost a bit of a wink to Amira. "Well get you in ASAP."

The clerk looks through the book to find us a room on the ground floor. "Cash this evening," asks the clerk.

Yes, that is fine, I say, with great respectability.

"Good, good. And, of course, the military discount."

My eyebrows go up. I look at Amira.

I do not look military. My hair is short, but not overly. I have a mustache. I am dressed in a t-shirt and jeans. Amira is wearing a cute dress with flowers and a denim jacket. I wonder, what is the tableau the clerk sees? The clerk continues smiling, waiting for my answer.

That will be fine, I say, stiffening my spine a bit to add some military-ness to my respectability.

He tells me a price that is 30% less than what we expect to pay. I hand over the money and he gives me the key.

"Good luck," says the clerk.

Not Sleep well. Not Goodnight. Good luck?

We find the room and unlock it. Amira goes to the parking lot to bring everyone else to the room via the side door. For some reason, Dex and Simon feel compelled to climb through the window of the room as if sneaking in—though for as much noise as they make, there is very little sneak accomplished. When all nine of us are in the room, I relay what happened while checking in.

"Prostitute," says Orla.

Everyone laughs except me.

What, I ask.

"Amira is your prostitute," explains Orla.

I recall the tableau at the front desk again. Young fellow, who apparently passes for military, with a cute girl next to him trying overly hard to look like a couple.

"It got us thirty percent off. I don't mind," says Amira.

"Thirty percent," exclaims Dex.

I divide evenly what remains of the pooled money between the group. The rest of the evening is spent talking and laughing. Somewhere close to midnight I start to think about what is next. Not the drive back home, but what might lie beyond. Drifting off, I feel resolved to find out.

The next morning, Natasha and I drive back to Anchorage. Everyone else plans to stay in Fairbanks a few more days, but both Natasha and I have to work. I have no idea how they will manage to stay with as much money remains between them.

It is a six- to seven-hour drive from Fairbanks to Anchorage. Miles do not matter here—in Alaska, distance is judged by time. Almost always it is how many car hours or, if it is somewhere in the Bush, plane hours.

We leave at 6am and pass by the main gate to *Elmendorf* almost exactly six hours later. I think about my military discount and laugh. I am so very far away from what the military would want. I drop Natasha at APU and drive along 36th to A St, then a right on Benson and into the *Cafe del Mundo* parking lot. It is still about a half hour until my shift starts. I sit at the counter, order coffee and a croissant, and by the time I finish both, I still have 15 minutes before my shift.

I look over my shoulder at the one-way window that allows people in the office to look out into the main room. I push my dishes toward the edge of the counter and decide now is the time. I walk into the office. Perry is there going over receipts and other paperwork. I give notice.

"Okay," replies Perry.

He says it as someone who is not quite listening, but agrees to what has just been said. Except, I know he heard me. I suspect he is a bit relieved at the idea of being rid of me.

The rest of my shift goes by as usual. Absolutely No Caffeine Woman comes in for her daily. Several people who are air-quote important come in as Midtown *del Mundo* is, for some reason, the place to be for the quasi- to exceedingly-rich.

A few people who are actually important come in, such as two of The Lesbians Three. I tell Joan and Natalie about giving notice. They are happy for me, but Joan cuts to the chase.

"Who will you recommend and train to make our drinks correctly since you won't be here?"

Classic Joan. Always asking the obvious and most important questions.

Let me have a think, I tell her.

I do understand where her question comes from. There are plenty of people behind this bar, and coffee bars all over town, who I would not like to have making my drinks.

Over the next 5 hours, I drink entirely too much espresso. I am vibrating. After my shift, I sit at one of the tables with my seventh espresso. My right hand shakes as I raise the cup to my lips. It is possible I have too much caffeine in me as my left hand begins to press through the table with very little resistance. Perry walks over with purpose and sits next to me, visibly in a bit of a huff.

"What's this Stan tells me," he asks.

At first I do not follow. Partly because I exist in a new plane of reality where my body can move through solid objects because I am vibrating so quickly. Partly also because Perry's question is such a non-sequitur. Until it is not. Stan. I know a Stan, I manage to think to myself. I pull disparate memories to my oscillating position in this current space-time. He...is the person for whom I used my employee discount to get a super fancy espresso machine. That is likely what Perry is on about.

What, I ask, as I am pulled back to this plane of existence.

"Stan said to me earlier that he was sorry for his part in getting you moved here," continues Perry.

He looks at me expectantly.

I start to put more than two and two together, really getting the hang of this thinking cogently stuff. I realize that Perry thinks I lied to him. I realize, based on how Stan phrased his apology, I did lie to Perry. Technically. Ish. Not at all with malicious intent. We are only supposed to use our employee discount for ourselves. Stan did get a discount, but I covered the difference. I try taking Perry's perspective into account, but it does not seem like anything to get upset about—he got all the money.

I spend the next several minutes assuring Perry that what Stan meant to say was that he felt responsible, not that I lied. Eventually, Perry seems to see my perspective. He is still upset, but there is no huff left in him. As he rises from the chair he says, "Don't worry about two weeks. One week is fine."

Okay. Still a little huff left it seems.

OVER the following week, I introduce Sherry to The Lesbians Three.

Sherry has already noticed Natalie in a "she's real perdy"-way and seems happy to be anointed as the cafe's primary representative to royalty. I show Sherry how I make drinks, which, for some reason, is different from everyone else who works here.

I show her the Hot-n-Cold: Cold milk on the bottom, hot, foamy milk on top, espresso in the middle. I show her the Lollygagger: a latte with quarter shots of almond and hazelnut syrups and cinnamon and nutmeg brewed with the espresso. I show her how to make a mocha properly: powdered Ghirardelli chocolate steamed with the milk—none of this syrup in the glass mixed up after pouring in the coffee crap that so many cafes seem to do.

This seems to please Their Highnesses, praise be their names, and it gives Sherry multiple excuses to talk to Natalie.

I also give my notice to Stan, who apologizes again. I half feel like my disappearance from Downtown *del Mundo* has upset the balance of customers' ability to get good drinks. Stan waves his hand at my notice. "All good, man. We hired someone full time and won't have much need for you anyway."

Done and done, I suppose.

The two weeks leading up to my departure are exhausting. I keep running into people I have not seen in a long time. It is disquieting—as though they are popping into my life to say goodbye for the final time.

I run into Terry at the sushi counter at *Carr's* two nights before I leave. He was one of my teachers in high school. We talk for roughly ten minutes, shifting back and forth to let customers up to the counter to order sushi or pick up a tray of the pre-made stuff. He asks how I am doing and what my plans are for the future. He tells me about himself and his wife Suzy, who was also a teacher of mine—one who saved me from failing out of school and helped me when all the other adults in my life would not and did not.

I feel him eating every word I say, as if he is hungry for a diversion. He shares concern and excitement about my plans. He gives a few suggestions of places to visit in the Lower 48—should I find myself near them—then ends our conversation with a quick psychoanalysis as we make our way to the checkout lines. "I'll pass along to Suzy, verbatim, all the things you shared. Even the non-verbal things. Everything looks good. This is the happiest I've ever seen you."

I leave him at the checkout stand, feeling both upset for the analysis and relief that a proper grown-up approves of my plan—what little there is of it. As a wise person has said, "While it is always best to believe in one's self, a little help from others can be a great blessing." If I do not actually believe in myself, I suppose I should take it where I can get it.

After paying, I leave and walk across the to the far side of the parking lot. There are so many cars here that the only place to park is along Northern Lights. The cacophonous rush of the traffic feels overwhelming until I get in the car and close the door. I set my small grocery bag on the seat next to me, put the key in the ignition, then...do nothing. I give an audible *huh* of realization. It feels good to have someone's approval. That is likely why I tell each person I run into about my plans. I am hoping the people I appreciate will tell me what I am doing is the right thing to do.

And perhaps, in a way, I am looking for permission to leave. Permission from found family and friends, and even from people I see every day but do not actually know—like the better customers at *del Mundo*.

I am unsure of my plan and unsure of myself. Everyone I tell says it all sounds wonderful and they wish me well. "Go for it," and "Good luck," they tell me as they walk away to go about their day. No one stands in front of me, keeping me from going through the next door.

Is that not what is supposed to happen, I ask myself aloud, reaching for the key to start up the car. Surely someone is supposed to Threshold Guardian me.

I know without needing anyone to tell me, that the only way to find out who I am or where I am going in life, is to take a deep breath and "Go that way, really fast. If something gets in your way...turn", as is taught to all students of Charles de Mar, true hero of the movie *Better Off Dead*.

Here on the veritable island of Alaska, I feel stifled—I feel a need to get out of my rut. Though I am unsure if I would have noticed had Meg not said anything. Perhaps that is what Terry means by the non-verbal stuff—that I understand the purpose of this trip, or, at least, I am beginning to understand it—even if I cannot yet articulate it.

I pull out of the parking spot and onto Northern Lights, and enter the flow of rush hour traffic—which seems to be every hour in Anchorage. Twenty minutes later, I walk into an empty house and begin to pack for travel.

I meet Molly at ANC in front of the Alaska Airlines ticket counter where she pays to change the travel date to today. We go through metal detectors at security, walk to the gate, and sit together on the hard, plastic chairs across from the gate.

I find it difficult to think of things to talk about. I dislike flying enough that most of my attention is on the things that can, but will likely not, go wrong. It does not take long for the flight crew to announce that it is time for boarding.

"Okay, Molly," says Molly with an emphasis on her name. "Have an excellent trip."

I tell her I will, even though I am not sure I will.

Molly gives me a hug. I thank her again for the ticket as she walks away from the gate. I board the plane, find my seat, and start my ritual to get set for take off. I put the blanket around my legs and tuck it beneath me so that my legs cannot easily move about. As I reach between the wall of the plane and the chair to get the other half of the seat belt, the guy sitting next to me gently taps my arm. I turn my head quickly, expecting some sort of confrontation over the armrest, but he nods to the aisle. I look up and one of the flight attendants is looking at me as though she has been trying to get my attention.

"Excuse me, sir," says the attendant.

The jig is up. They know I am not Molly.

"Are you supposed to be in that seat?"

Wow, I think to myself, they really do know.

I think so, I stammer.

I hand my ticket to her. She looks it over.

"Yep, 12-A," she says, confirming I am in the correct seat. "Looks like two people got the same seat. I'll reassign you, sir," she says to the man standing next to her. She looks at me, back at the ticket, then hands the ticket to me.

"Have a nice trip...ma'am."

I smile at her and relax back in my seat, thankful the jig is not up.

The plane fills with people going on trips to Seattle and points beyond. I look out the window and watch the ground crew do a mix of careful and not-so-careful baggage handling. I listen to the *clunks* of doors being closed. I feel the air coming out of the funnel above my head—it smells like not-quite-clean air. I think about what I am going toward and what I am going away from and I cannot decide if there is more toward or more away-from.

I think it must be healthier to go toward things. But after I arrive at SEA, I do not know what I will go toward. So the bulk of why I am sitting in this seat must be a lot of away-from reasons.

Away from Perry and Midtown *del Mundo*. Away from family. Away from friends. Away from mosquitoes the size of eagles. Away from car-destroying volcanoes. Away from yet another winter, as I can see earlier-each-year Termination Dust on the foothills from the window of the plane. Away from my connection to anything high school or university. Away from books in a library. Away from scheduled work. Away from this weird island.

I will miss some things: Dinners at the big table at *Simon's*. Lunches at *Sacks*. Coffee at *Kaladi*. Movies at *Capri*. But in this moment, in this seat, impersonating Molly, I am quite happy to feel the *rumble-hum* of the plane's engines as they spin up to taxi away from the gate.

Meg is right. Time to make a move. Whatever that ends up looking like.

Time to scatter to Seattle.

SEATTLE

Only when I'm dancing can I feel this free
At night I lock the doors, where no one else can see
I'm tired of dancing here all by myself
Tonight I want to dance with someone else

—Madonna

THE chest-thudding club music fades from overwhelming to an almost sub-audible drone as the bathroom door closes, but the damage is done—the song is burned indelibly into my brain. I find myself singing along with it under my breath.

I approach the urinal, unzip, and start peeing. It is such a relief after so many beers and, again, to my surprise, dancing. We do not talk about this enough—sometimes peeing is wonderful.

The guy next to me, in the same here-on-business stance, starts to turn my direction. It becomes apparent immediately that he and I are not here on the same business. He has an erection and a look on his face that communicates an invitation to partake.

No thanks, man, I say, politely, and finish up.

I leave the bathroom much less a fan of uninvited erections than before. Madonna. Dancing. Mostly men. Why did the women I am staying with for a couple of days bring me to a gay bar?

I wind my way across the dance floor as if it is an obstacle course and try to make it look like dancing as I go. I sit back down with Marie and Sandy at one of the few four-top tables in the place—we are on the periphery of joyously-flung sweat.

Gay bar, I ask, raising my voice to be heard over the DJ playing the intro to *Wall of Voodoo's Dance You Fuckers* as she riles up the crowd for the next number.

"Yes! The best," answers Sandy. "When you move to a new city you need to go to the most popular gay bar, if they have one. They're the mostest fun."

It is fun, but I prefer less penis when I go out, I yell.

"I hear that," yells Marie, raising her wine glass in toast.

I tell them of my experience in the bathroom tho which Marie responds, "Welcome to Seattle?"

The urinal is a sacred space, I explain to them.

"Leave penis sharing to the stalls," says Sandy. She's resting her head on her hand, trying to keep from listing to one side.

"I am not sure if that needs to be in an advice column or book on etiquette, but clearly there is some wider ratification of this clause of the social contract to be done," says Marie.

We stay only a few minutes longer as the DJ has left the stage and put a playlist on to cover for her. On the way back to their place, we wander the streets of Capitol Hill. I feel as if we are walking in circles and, after we pass the same flower shop for the second time, I realize that we are. I ask and Marie explains they prefer to "walk off the liquor" before heading home. We walk up and down the block a few times, then up 10th, across Pine, and into the park. The sun has long since set, but there is plenty of city light by which to see.

"I'm not going to make it," says Sandy as she bends over behind a bench in front of the reflecting pool.

"You couldn't have done this back by the trees," asks Marie.

She sounds exasperated and concerned. Sandy's cancer treatments ended 10 months ago, but I can tell each time something like this happens— wow, that is very audible retching—Marie gets worried. Tonight though, it seems that it was one-too-many Gin and Tonics.

I sit a few benches away from the smell as Sandy recovers and Marie holds her hair back. I think about the amount someone needs to care about another human to hold their hair while they empty out booze and sushi behind a bench in a public park at two in the morning. The amount is a lot.

Sandy eventually gets her wind back and the three of us walk back to their place on the corner of 11th and Harrison. It is a cute place, with bright yellow paint and a welcoming garden in front. I bid them goodnight and walk down the stairs into the basement to the space they set up for me, in the middle of the detritus of twenty years of two people living together.

The pull-out couch is serviceable in that it is mostly flat where needed. There are sheets hung around it with tiny, faded, yellow daisies to give a semblance of privacy. I feel lucky that there is also a toilet and sink down here. It is now, technically, my second day in Seattle and I feel as though I have been here a week.

I deem it a good visit, exceptions made for uninvited penises.

The following morning, I wake with Madonna's music still ringing in my ears and a strange determination for pancakes. I make the bed and walk up the creaking steps to the main floor, directly into the kitchen. Marie is pouring coffee into a cup and hands it to me before I can even croak out a request. I take a sip and let the healing power of the bean flow through me.

It is enough that I am able to make my request, without croaking.

I want pancakes, I say.

"You do not," says Marie.

I feel like I do, I say.

"You want Dutch Babies," she proclaims.

Now, I am all for exploring the world, but I am not ready to have children, I say.

"Souffle pancakes. Pancakes, but better, basically," Sandy clarifies.

Okay. I want that, I say.

"Yer damn right," says Marie. "We'll leave in a few and walk over. It's roughly a thirty minute walk, but it's super nice out. We need to get there before they open so we can sit at the bar."

Another bar, I ask as I drink more coffee and the music from last night rings in my ears.

"Yer damn right," exclaims Marie.

Sandy winces. It seems the music still rings in her ears as well.

I finish my coffee, grab my wandering bag from the basement, and join Marie and Sandy in their front yard. The sun hits my back and, while not quite warm yet, teases the heat that is coming. We gather ourselves after Sandy locks the door and off we walk.

Marie and Sandy lead the way. They hold hands and swing their arms as if they are about to skip away over the horizon. I walk alone, behind them, as skipping is entirely too far a reach for me this morning. Down Harrison, left on Broadway, and right along the curve of Olive until we switch to Denny where we stay for the next 20 minutes. The day is decidedly warming up, but the shady bits are still quite cool—I wish for a jacket in them and am glad I do not have one in the sunny bits.

I let the two of them stay well ahead of me for most of the walk, but never lose sight. Sandy seems to want to talk to Marie privately and I give them the space to do so.

I notice them jaywalk across Denny. On the other side they turn to wave and wait for me. I catch up quickly, but still feel like I make them wait too long. Likely I left more room between us than needed. We turn left and after a block, walking a shady path beneath the fully-leaved trees, we arrive at *Tilikum Place Cafe*.

"Crap," says Marie.

There is already quite a line. We stand around for roughly 40 minutes before we are ushered in. We could have gone in within 10 minutes, but someone named Marie wants us to sit at the bar—there are only six seats there and it takes a while to get three next to each other.

These souffle pancakes had better be worth it, I say.

"Hush, you," says Marie.

We sit on the high-back stools and each attempt to shuffle them into place so we are not too far from the bar itself. Elbow room is at a premium. Both at the bar and everywhere in here. It is almost as loud and crowded as last night, though the music is not as penetrating and the restroom is likely more reserved.

Sandy hands the menus back to the server the moment he sets them down.

"Three regular Dutch Babies, please. Also, coffee. Lots and lots of coffee."

"Dutch Babies take twenty minutes to make. You up for that? Want anything while you wait," asks the server.

"Coffee. Lots and lots of coffee," repeats Sandy, with an emphasis that asks rhetorically if she mumbled the first time she said it.

Away goes the server and soon we are provided with coffee and coffee accouterments. I am not a fan of coffee accouterments, but Sandy is. She seems to essentially make herself a latte with the amount of milk she puts in. Marie and I take it black.

Thankfully, the server took Sandy seriously about the coffee, for we did not want for it over what turned out to be a thirty-minute wait.

Eventually, three servers file out from the kitchen and then behind the bar, as if they are in a parade. I hear someone ask, "What is that," as they walk by. In unison, each cast iron skillet is set before us with...a souffle pancake. Powdered sugar adorns most of it and there is a large wedge of lemon in the middle. It smells divine. One of the servers cautions us to the heat of the skillets, but I dig in before he finishes the sentence.

Worth the wait. Pancakes are dead to me, I think to myself with a mouthful of not-pancakes.

"Hey, Sandy," I hear from behind us.

"Hector, hey," replies Sandy, with a big smile on her face.

I turn my head, between mouthfuls, to see a young man standing behind Sandy and Marie. Sandy twists around to give him an awkward hug, almost hitting Marie in the process, who deftly dodges Sandy's elbow with what seems like a lot of lived experience.

They speak together for a moment—I cannot quite hear them—then Sandy says, "Oh, Hector. I am glad we ran into you today. This," she turns awkwardly in my direction—Marie prepares to dodge though it is not needed—, "is my friend from Alaska."

I am in the midst of taking a bite and raise my arm over Marie's head into his line of sight for a quick wave.

Pancakes are dead to me, I say as I finish chewing a mouthful.

"Rightly so," replies Hector.

He smiles warmly, seeing the Dutch Babies in front of us. I turn and go back to eating, assuming they will continue their conversation. But Sandy says, looking at me, "Say, Hector. What are you up to today?" Marie groans slightly under her breath.

"*Nada.* What you got," he asks.

"We're going to the Space Needle," she exclaims.

"Cool," says Hector, with a lack of surety as to why Sandy is telling him this seemingly amazing news. "I walked around there yesterday."

"Oh," says Sandy, a little disappointed.

Marie sighs. "Want to walk around it again," she asks, trying to move the conversation to the conclusion Sandy seems to want.

"Uh, sure, I guess. I got food to go anyway." He holds up a to-go bag in his left hand. "No plans today other than to eat this non-Dutch Baby. Might as well go over to the park and eat under the Needle."

"Great," says Sandy, perking up some and looking at me.

I did not know what we were up to today, beyond dethroning pancakes. I am up for whatever, I say.

"Great," says Sandy again with rising enthusiasm.

Hector chuckles, as does Marie.

"I'm going to head over there and find a conspicuous bench or something to sit on and eat. Catch me there when you're done," he says.

He waves and walks away as Sandy shouts, "We will!"

We finish up our breakfast and Marie pays.

I do have money, I say.

"Meh," replies Marie.

"Save it for the rest of the trip," says Sandy.

I shrug and thank them. We backtrack half a block and cross the street. I can see the Space Needle above the rooftops of the buildings in front of us. No idea why I did not notice it before as, based on how we got here, I should have. Too much time spent looking at my feet I suppose.

A quick left, then a right, and we are walking straight toward it. It does not take us long to get to the area immediately beneath the structure.

We can see Hector eating his food, sitting on a retaining wall that runs the length of the entrance into the park. We walk up, and Sandy and Marie sit on either side of him. I stand in front of them, mostly out of the way of passersby as the area fills with picnickers, children, and buskers. It feels crowded and loud, but we easily carry on a pleasant, essentially meaningless conversation as Hector eats his food. Sandy and Marie do most of the talking while I let my eyes wander around the park. I do not pay particular attention to them as it feels like I am interrupting their reunion, but I pick up that Hector comes to Seattle once a month for a long weekend, though I am not sure why. He mentions that he lives in Portland.

That is where I am going tomorrow, I say, inserting myself into the conversation.

"Cool," says Hector. "Me, too."

MONDAY. The day after what shall henceforth be known as *St Dutch*

Baby Day. This is the last day I am able to stay with Sandy and Marie—and also the only place I can stay for free in Seattle. They are off to the east coast for a work-related event for Marie.

"Work, then vacation," sighs Marie with heavy, relieved emphasis on the word vacation.

I pack my things, what little I have, into the solitary backpack I have with me. I pull the sheet off the bed and fold the blanket. The washables go in a pile in the middle of the bed and with that, I bid this memory-and-junk-cluttered basement goodbye.

Once upstairs, Sandy asks, "You sure we can't take you?"

No. It is only two miles and I can walk it easily enough. It is mostly downhill, I say.

It turns out to be mostly uphill somehow. This is my eleventieth trip to Seattle and I am still surprised by how hilly it is. I walk the bulk of the way south on Broadway to James, then cut left on 6th to parallel the eye- and ear-sore that is Interstate 5. I am about to turn on Jackson when I see a bank clock and realize I am much earlier than I need to be for the Shin to Portland.

I stay on Sixth and find myself standing in front of *A+ Hong Kong Kitchen*. I realize I am hungry as all I took for breakfast was coffee. The scents of ginger, cloves, star anise, and garlic assault my nose and I welcome it. With A+ in the name, it must be good, I think to myself. And also, apparently, say it out loud, which prompts a couple leaving the restaurant to respond with surety, "It's very good."

The best way to find good food is to take the advice of total strangers.

I enter and sit in a chair near the door. The place is packed and loud, but the smells remind me of home—even though Anchorage doesn't smell like this. I feel somewhat nostalgic as I scan the room watching servers deliver plates and bowls heaped with steaming food. I hear someone yell, *mái dān*, and tilt my head at an almost-memory as if I can sense a past experience I have not yet had. My reverie is interrupted by a menu being shoved into my hands.

"Thirty minute wait for a table. Five minute wait for to-go," says the woman.

She walks away before I fully parse the statement. I think about the time and decide to-go it is. I'm early enough to grab food, but not early enough to wait thirty minutes. I peruse the menu. Plenty of pictures help with the fact that the menu is in Cantonese with some English sprinkled here and there.

Every aspect of this place is A+ Hong Kong.

Within moments she is back with a *Well...* questioning look on her face. I tell her that I want it to-go and point at something titled *Mixed Vegetable Mala Tang or Sour & Spicy Noodle Soup*. I am not sure if I will get malatang or soup or...

"How hot," she asks, writing down my order.

Medium, I say, but it comes out more as a question.

She studies me for a moment, then approves of—or more likely allows—my choice with a curt nod. She finishes writing my order on a pad, grabs the menu, then says, "ten." As first I am not sure if she means ten minutes or ten dollars. She faces the pad toward me and repeats herself.

I take out my wallet and hand her a ten dollar bill. She takes it and looks at me, barely moving. I take out two more dollars and hand them over. Again, I get a curt nod of approval and she is off.

It takes less than five minutes to get my food, which she hands to me wrapped in a plastic bag.

"Okay," she says as a goodbye.

To which I respond, *m goi*, though I am not entirely sure how or why I know to say that.

Again, the curt nod of approval, but this time with a very, very slight smile.

There is a park across the street and I can see many people sitting on benches, the ground, some planters even. Several people stroll through. It is essentially lunch time, and the bulk of the people I can see who are not wandering through are also eating.

I walk across the street and sit on a retaining wall near the intersection. I untie the plastic bag and see a container of red liquid with vegetables and a container with rice. I am unsure this is what I ordered, but it smells like I brought the restaurant with me.

I open the container with the red liquid, careful to not spill it, and take a sip. My mouth is immediately on fire, both from the heat of the soup and from the spices. I question the rationale of allowing restaurants to use words like Medium to describe spice level as I put the lid back on and close up the plastic bag.

Two men walk past and one says, "We better walk quickly if we want to get back in time." This prompts me to look for a clock. There isn't one. I ask a person sitting across from me on the other retaining wall for the time. It is close enough to when boarding will start that I should make my way to the station.

I walk back to Jackson, down to Second, and around to the main entrance of the station. A rainbow procession of cabs loops slowly between me and the doors. I make my way between them and enter the building. The place is almost as crowded as the A+ restaurant. Which makes me think of the food I have and how I am craving more even though I only had one sip. Excellent spicy food has that kind of hold on me.

Of the six service counters, five are Amtrak and one is for the Shin, which is what I am taking to Portland. Why ride for three and a half hours when I can do it in one? It is twice the price of an Amtrak ticket, but so very worth it to be more efficient with time—assuming the placards and brochures which surround me are telling the truth.

I ask for a seat in one of the Quiet Cars. I take four twenties out of my wallet and hand them to the clerk. He hands me my ticket and admonishes me to wait in the area as boarding will begin soon.

"The train leaves promptly at one-twenty. With or without you."

He says it with the confidence of someone relating that gravity exists.

I shall endeavor to seek not distractions which may tarry me, I reply.

He is not impressed with my fake Shakespeare and calls out for the next customer.

I take a brochure and wander over to the windows which look south, down the track. I can see several trains, including the Shin and can barely make out the roof line of the *Kingdome* from this vantage. I decide to sit on the floor in front of the window.

I set down my backpack and my bag of Cantonese cuisine. As I am about to sit, I look to my left and see a payphone. It prompts me to think about home.

I reach into the left, front pocket of my jeans and find two quarters. I take one out. It is dull and has been in circulation for so long I cannot make out the minting date. But it will suffice for a call. I pick up the receiver, drop in the coin, and start to dial that familiar nine-zero-seven number. The sound of an outgoing call replaces the clicking sound of the rotary dial.

One ring. Two rings. No answer.

One xylophone note. Two xylophone notes. A pleasant voice issues from the speakers in the ceiling. "Boarding for the Shinkansen to Portland, Oregon will commence presently. Please exit the waiting area through door six and proceed to your assigned carriage."

Five rings. No answer. I hang up and put my finger in the coin tray to retrieve my quarter, except there is nothing there. The phone ate my quarter.

Time to make a move.

I walk through the door marked six, then along the Shin to toward the far end of the train from the station. I show my ticket to the conductor. He waves me in as if I am late to arrive. I step up and to my right and am immediately blocked by someone who crouches in the aisle in front of me.

I tilt my head to one side and watch him, trying to discern what he is up to. There is no one immediately ahead of him, though at the far end of the car there are several people putting luggage above the seats and standing in the aisle themselves.

As I begin to ask him to move, there is a flash of light and I hear the familiar *click-clack-whirr-snap* of a Polaroid being taken. The person stands up, turns around, and says, "*Lo siento*," then trails off. He smiles. "*Hola.*"

It is Hector.

I squint my eyes a bit. A habit of mine when I am trying to understand something.

Hector asks, "*¿Qué pasa?*"

My seat, I reply, and give a nod down the aisle.

Hector laughs with a ready smile. "*Sí, sí...*"

He lets the camera drop from his hand, to be caught by the cord around his neck, and picks up his small bag. He turns around and walks down the aisle, finding his seat in the middle of the carriage, next to the window.

I follow and find that my seat is two rows back from him on the other side. He smiles at me again as I pass. I put my bag on the rack above my seat and settle into the extremely comfortable chair next to the window.

There are people outside walking toward the end of the train, while others walk the opposite direction as an Amtrak pulled into the station a few minutes prior. They jumble and weave. For some reason, it makes me think of salmon going upriver and that a large contingency of the fish have decided, "You know what, screw the river. I prefer the ocean." Roller bags collide, glares exchange, but somehow everyone finds their way forward, regardless of whichever direction is forward for them.

After a few more minutes, the conductor starts his patrol through the carriage. It is times like this, I think about the video game *Castle Wolfenstein* and the guards demanding, "*Aus pass!*" Brains are odd.

I hear him asking for people's tickets, as well as adding on something else. Eventually he is near enough for me to hear, "Ticket? The train is running light today. Once we start to pull away, feel free to sit anywhere in this carriage."

I look over at Hector. The conductor turns to him and repeats the message. There are three people between me and Hector; two sitting directly in front of me, and one sitting behind him. I can tell there is no one in the seats opposite him and no one next to him. I can feel my anxiety rising. The conductor moves forward, again repeating the message, and I watch Hector start to turn his head toward me, then stop and turn back to looking out the window.

I sigh. I feel like a nice long—okay, short—ride on a fast train, alone, is something to look forward to. I am beginning to suspect I will not be able to sit alone. The conductor gets to me. I hand him my ticket and before he can speak, I quickly say to him what he has said ten times already.

He nods and marks my ticket, then before handing it back to me, gives me his spiel. I roll my eyes. He smiles and moves on.

I sit for a bit longer, my attention behind me as I mouth the words the conductor is saying to each and every person. The train gives me a gentle bump and I look out the window to see we are moving and am relieved to find that I am not sitting backwards, even though that feels like it should be safer.

I look up and see Hector looking back at me. Our eyes meet and I can tell by the shape of his that he is smiling. He waves. I nod back and look out the window again. I do not want to leave this seat, I tell myself. And yet, moments later, I find myself getting up, grabbing my backpack, and walking up two rows to stand in the aisle next to Hector. The brief walk up is a bit disorientating as I am walking against the direction of the train and, for a moment, it feels like I am standing still even though I can tell I am moving.

I put my bag on the rack above the seats across the aisle from Hector. I look at him then back at the seats under my backpack. It will be too odd if I move twice.

This seat taken, I ask.

Hector holds out his hand, palm up, and gestures to the seat offering it to me.

It is only an hour... Fifty-nine minutes now. I do my best to smile at him and sit.

Heading home, I ask, at minute fifty-eight.

I try to keep my voice light, as if I want to be sitting next to him. I do not feel there is anything wrong with Hector, but I was looking forward to not having to be on for a while.

"*Sí. Estaba visitando a mi papi*," replies Hector. Then, with a quiet chuckle, "Sorry, man. With the exception of when we met yesterday, I've been speaking only Spanish the past few days. Sometimes I don't shift quickly."

That's alright. I can understand *sí*, I say.

He crooks his head to one side, exaggerating the gesture, and adds an incredulous look.

Okay, okay. I also got visit and your dad. Good enough to get the picture, I explain.

He laughs, "Cool," lifting his head back up.

Desafortunadamente, my Spanish is incredibly rusty, I say.

His incredulous look returns.

Fifty-seven minutes.

The train starts to pick up speed as we dive under the city for the first section of the trip. I take a brochure out of the seat pocket in front of me. I unfold it to show an illustrated history of the Shin. This one seems to be intended for children. Somewhere around Kent, we will resurface. Until that point, I assume my ears will keep popping.

As there is no scenery to look at, and the illustrated brochure is short, I ask Hector what brings him to Seattle. I sound almost like someone who can carry on a conversation with another human. Masking can be useful, I suppose.

"I come up once a month for a long weekend," he explains. "Primarily to visit my," he pauses a moment, drops the slight accent, and says in a very bland American accent, "father." He really draws it out, too.

You can say, *papi*. I truly can understand some Spanish, I tell him.

He laughs, returning to his regular accent. "No worries, man. I'm playing."

You come up just to visit him, I ask.

"Yeah," he answers, and seems to communicate that he is done talking about it with a tight smile.

I nod. I have some family in Seattle, but this trip I am only passing through, I say.

"How long are you staying in Portland," asks Hector.

No idea. Until they kick me out or it is time to move on, I say.

He nods.

Fifty-four minutes.

We sit in silence for the next few minutes, then a pleasant chime rings throughout the train as the interior lights dim and raise a few times. We then blast out of the tunnel and sunlight floods the carriage. I squint again. No sunglasses. It takes a moment for my eyes to adjust. I look over to Hector who is looking out the window.

Forty-eight minutes.

I feel like I need to say something, but my brain stumbles along unable to think of anything to bring up. Hector shifts in his seat and the camera around his neck slides to one side to knock against the armrest. He looks at it and moves it back into his lap.

Cah-mer-uh, my brain offers. Yes, I could ask about the camera. Nice one, brain.

Have you been taking pictures long, I ask.

My brain beams with approval.

Hector pulls his gaze from the outside world that bends behind us. "Yeah, for a while now. I have a few cameras, but this is the one I take with me to Seattle."

I nod, attempting to encourage more details.

"Mostly I paint, though," he adds.

Oh, cool, I say. What kinds of things do you paint or take pictures of, I ask.

My brain beams again. I want to give him as much room to work with as possible so that he can do all the talking and all I have to do is mostly listen and look out the window.

"Lately, I've been taking pictures of obstacles, or more accurately, people being obstacles. Never faces. I never want to see a face in a picture I take. So I crop when I shoot, or after, or I'll smudge out their face when I am developing, if I'm not using the Polaroid. I want people to be able to look at it and think it could be them. It's not that I'm not interested in faces, I love to paint them, but when I take pictures, I dunno...just don't want to see them. It's too personal. Paint is a level of abstraction. If I paint you, everyone can see it's you, but it sort of isn't. With photography, it's you. But that isn't what I am interested in capturing. Not exactly anyway."

Thirty-nine minutes. Trees wisp by out the window.

I nod. Painting, too, I ask.

"Sure," he says. "Mostly what I do. I tend to paint people who aren't people but also they are." He smiles a little as I give him a look. "You have to see it. I have a lot of work, but I'm not showing anywhere, so I suppose it will be hard to see and I should get better at explaining it. But for now..."

He lets the thought drift away.

Thirty-eight.

Do you want something to drink, I ask. I feel the need for some coffee and would be happy to get you one.

"Sure, man," he answers.

I get up and walk the wrong direction at first, then double back, past my seat, then three cars back toward Seattle. The dining car, if it can be called that, has some seating on one side, looking out the window, and six vending machines on the other side. I choose the BOSS coffee machine, which yells at me with its allcaps name.

I slide in two dollars and select two cans of Rainbow Blend. Both cans roll out hot and I walk back to my seat. Hector is not there. I pull down the tray and set his can in the cup holder. I open my very colorful can and am immediately lambasted with a bitter coffee aroma. I take a tentative sip. It is bitter. And hot. And is exactly what I want in this moment.

I watch the trees and towns *swoosh* by and wish I were sitting on my own. I wish I did not have to sit with Hector. There is nothing wrong with him at all, but I can feel my arm sliding into a familiar coat sleeve—one I wear from time to time. The coat keeps me away from people. Currently, one arm is part way into the sleeve. I know I don't have to put the coat on, but it feels comfortable when I am uncomfortable. It feels familiar when I am not. I am not exactly sure why it is a coat, but that is what it feels like—where I can feel it physically.

Thirty-one minutes.

The problem with the coat is that I am entering a time where connecting with others, in a place I have never been, will be important. I know this intellectually, but my brain does not seem to want to cooperate with the rest of me. I tell myself, your arm is only part of the way in, plenty of time still to take off the coat and stay awhile, as I take another sip of BOSS.

Hector returns, rubbing his hands together with sanitizer. The scent of which does not mix well with my BOSS coffee, but it does not linger long. I get up so he can reclaim his seat. He opens up his can, holds it up for a *tink*, and I oblige. We sip in silence for a bit. After a few more sips, my coffee is not as bitter tasting and I decide...I decide to stop paying attention to the time.

We talk a bit more about painting and photography. I explain my fear of blank canvases and he lets me know that my fear is not unique and is also understandable.

After a while, the Shin causes my body to lean forward briefly. Seconds later, a peaceful chime sounds, then an announcement that we are arriving at Portland. The announcement reminds us that it will be roughly ten minutes until we are able to disembark. The announcement also reminds us to gather all of our belongings.

I do not have much to gather and neither does Hector. There is barely any coffee in either of our cans and we sit in silence for the next few minutes.

As we start crossing a bridge, Hector asks, "Which quadrant?"

Which what now, I ask.

"Quadrant. Which one are you staying in?"

I am not sure, I say.

I stand to take a notebook out of the outer pocket of my bag on the shelf above. As I sit again, I remove the strap and open to the first page.

The address is on Northwest Flanders, I say.

I put together the word Quadrant with Northwest and give an *ahhh* of understanding.

Northwest Quadrant, I say.

"What address," he asks.

The address is 2015, I say.

"Damn, man. That's an expensive area," says Hector.

I am staying with someone I know for a little while. A few days, maybe a week, I explain.

Hector nods, "That's cool. Wasn't sure if you were moving there or what. It's a nice area, but the prices are steep. Though there are some places with good, cheap food."

I'm willing to pay for good food, but definitely prefer to not pay for good food, I say.

I smile at my very small joke. Likely the first genuine smile all day. Hector returns it.

"S'cool, man. No judgment. I can't afford to live there, but I like going over now and then."

Where do you...Which quadrant, I ask. I feel proud that I am getting the local lingo down.

"Southeast. Kinda far out, but still technically in Portland."

Is it nice, I ask.

"Yeah, I mean, I can afford it. So, yeah, it's nice. It isn't shitty, how about that?"

I shrug. No judgment, I say, mimicking him. I don't know Portland, so it's all new to me.

The Shin is moving very slowly now. I look out the window and see a red bridge. We are barely moving as we go beneath it. Then, with another train-induced lean forward, we stop. Again a pleasant chime and an announcement welcoming us to Portland.

Everyone stands up to collect their things. Unlike the airplane experience, we do not get in each other's way, especially since there are not many passengers in the carriage.

Hector slings his camera so that it rests against his left hip, grabs his small bag, and gestures to me to lead the way. We disembark to see porters carrying luggage and pushing carts. Someone waves us to a pathway that is painted bright blue, which leads into *Union Station*.

Once inside, Hector says, "Well, man, good to chat with you. Hope you enjoy your time here."

I will, I say. And I am glad for our chat as well.

I realize I mean it.

"Cool. You know how to get where you're going? It's not far really. You're on the right side of the river."

I am good. I will figure it out, I say.

"Alright, man. Catch you on the flip side. Maybe we'll cross paths again."

Hector holds onto the loops of his bag and tosses it over his shoulder. He walks away from me, toward the main doors, with a no-look wave.

I make my way over to the ticketing counter to find a map of Portland. The kiosk is bare except for fliers announcing any number of local events. The tallest stack of which is something about *No On 9*, which I do not understand.

I ask someone where Twentieth and Flanders is, which opens me up to an explanation of, "Portland is a grid system. Mostly." Followed by, "that way to get to Flanders. Turn right and walk to Twentieth."

Simple enough.

I thank him and begin my walk to Cairene's place.

PORTLAND

No matter where you go... there you are.

—Confucius or Buckaroo Banzai. Same diff.

IT is Monday.

It may be Wednesday.

I do not know what the date is. For all I know, October is here and not knowing does not bother me one bit. I have not seen a newspaper for a while and have no idea what is going on outside my small world.

Cairene is not around, but her stuff is sitting on her art table. She always takes her black, "has my life in it," book with her, so I assume she will return soon. I lay on the fold-out futon couch and think about all the things I can do today. Nothing much comes to mind. The idea of taking a shower is as far as I get by the time Cairene comes back. She is carrying a load of clean laundry and greets me with a reserved tone.

Besides a muted greeting and a "back at five" goodbye, she does not say much else to me over the next twenty minutes. Today marks a week staying with her. I think. It could be a month gone at this point and I am enjoying my time staying with her less and less. I like her very much. She is a friend from Anchorage and, while I appreciate the place to flop, I hate feeling like I am underfoot.

I decide to get ready for my daily outing. My only choices are to leave or to stay as I have no key—once I am out, I am out. But it is a nice day so that will not be so bad.

While I shower and dress, I think about my next destination, not for today, but for the days to come. The next place I can stay for free is in Santa Fe. That is a long, painful bus ride from here. But, there is a free-to-use Ducati Paso waiting for me in San Francisco, not that I can ride it legally. Before I left Anchorage, one of the good regulars at Midtown *del Mundo* made the offer for me to use it should I make it that far.

I grab my notebooks, my pens, and my wallet and decide to think about this later. Things are too...mushy right now—my brain and the possibilities. Now it is time for sun, time to read, time to coffee, and time to write.

I step out of the building onto Flanders and walk toward 21st. I have a letter to send to Sherry. It is an excerpt from a book I am reading. The post office is only sixteen blocks from Cairene's place and that feels like an easy stroll. Walking to get somewhere is a new thing for me. In Anchorage, the town is so spread out that you have to drive everywhere. In Portland, I am forced to walk—no bike, too many people in Publics, and I cannot afford Shares. Walking is easier to start and stop than most modes of transport. You do not get as far, but the time spent is more interesting. I did not like walking at first, but now, it is growing on me.

The day is already hot and I welcome the short bursts of cool breeze and the shade of the trees along the sidewalk. I walk along 21st, then left at NW Northrup to 24th. Not far from the capitalistic trenches along 23rd and 21st, the houses along the mostly-residential 24th are good characters. All of them old, some kept up, some run down.

I walk past a restaurant called The Stepping Stone. I see a red-haired woman wearing an apron with the restaurant's logo standing in the threshold of the front door. She reminds me of someone, but I cannot recall who. I realize I have come to a stop to look at her while I try to place her face, even though I know I do not know her. She looks at me as she steps onto the sidewalk to clear away some dishes from the outside tables. We both smile and continue our separate ways.

I cross the street, past an enormous dirt lot that takes up an entire city block. Trees and bushes grow in and among the piles of dirt. Bicycle tire tracks can be seen going up and down the mounds. It looks almost like a purposeful dirt-sports event area, but thirty years after some apocalypse.

After mailing the letter to Sherry, I decide to walk aimlessly for a while. I arrive at 24th and Vaughn and the smell of industry hits me. The smell of burning rubber. A smell like ten thousand overworked copy machines. It stifles me. I turn back, walking down 23rd.

Clothing, coffee, knickknack, and bookstores. I go into three bookstores looking for *Blue Highways*, but not a copy to be found. The first store tells me that I will be hard-pressed to find a copy unless I try *Powell's*, but it is too hot to walk downtown and I have already walked a lot today.

At the register in the third bookstore, a woman comes in looking for a city map. Her skin is dark and smooth. Short brown hair, jeans cut off well above the knees, and eyes so bright and blue. She seems to be in desperate need of that map but, sadly, only has a hundred dollar bill with which to pay. The store cannot make change. Being the nice, friendly, suave, non-coat-wearing fellow I am trying to pretend to be, I offer to pay. With a small, and I mean small, amount of protest she accepts my offer, takes the map, and leaves. I finish my discussion with the bookstore people, "Like I said, try Powell's," and decide to find something to cool me down at The Place.

I call it The Place, but the real name is *The Renaissance Project*. It is a cafe and art gallery, more the former than the latter, but there is still an art show every month.

I ask for a drip cup of coffee, hoping the ancient idea of drinking something warm to cool off will work. The Necklace Man is the one behind the counter. He wears so very many necklaces—at least thirty—hence my sobriquet for him. Also, I do not know his name. He turns to the machine and grabs a portafilter with a long copper tube attached to the spout. I raise my eyebrows having not seen anything like this before.

He puts the portafilter under the grinder and fills it with fresh-ground coffee. He tamps it and runs it through the machine like an espresso, except the coffee comes pouring out of the copper tube into a tall glass sitting on the counter. When it is finished, there is very little crema.

He sets the coffee on the counter in front of me, asks if I want cream—I do not—and charges me one dollar, which I pay. I stand there a moment and take a sip. It tastes like a strong cup of coffee, somewhere between a drip and a French Press. I like it, and more, I like the way it is brewed-to-order. Especially for a slower shop. No airpot sitting on the counter with two-hour-old coffee in it that has to be thrown away because it is not fresh enough. So smart.

I decide to sit on the small stage at the back of the room. I assume this allows The Place to host live events, but currently there are a handful of tables placed up here. It is not very busy right now, but there is still an ambient buzz as most of the people here are in conversation.

After a few minutes enjoying this unique cup of coffee and staring out the window, Michael, one of the owners, comes over to sit with me. Apparently, I come here enough in my short or long time here that I rate sitting with the owner.

He talks about plans for future expansion next door. He wants to install a wood-fired pizza oven—who does not these days—with a small deli. The new space will serve to-go food only, but let people eat on this side. He talks about meeting with the architect, during which they got to talking about how the space has been used over the years.

"Before it was The Renaissance Project, it was a gay nightclub, but I don't recall the name. Before that it was a fish market that may have been part of *Durst's*, but I am not sure about that," explains Michael. "The architect said she'd look into it."

Eventually, Michael wanders off for another meeting with his contractor and I sit, downing my coffee, reading very little, writing none, and watching the world go by outside.

I spend the rest of the day walking in the heat and resting from walking in the heat. After a few hours, I become entirely too hot and go in search of shade with a good view. I walk up to the *Rose Test Gardens*. The gardens sit on a hill that look out over the city. It is nice to be somewhere the roses keep blooming past September. Assuming it is past September.

A tour bus shudders to a stop nearby. Moments later, a group of older Japanese people disembark and make their way into the garden. I watch them look at the flowers, take pictures, and enjoy the whole *Rose Test Garden* experience.

An older man, not with the group, in all-tan clothing with a cane, sits on a bench near me. He hacks and coughs for a moment, then spits into the roses. Several others seem to be playing hooky from work with their friends and lovers. Two children play in the penny fountain as their parents look on.

I sit on my bench, alone, in the shade, surrounded by people and roses.

Clouds attempt to cover us, but the sun burns them off. The bus reloads its tourists and departs. Another bus arrives moments later. The man in tan hobbles away. A woman in blue takes his place.

I close my eyes and feel the heat, even though the sun is beginning to slip behind the tall trees of the park. I can feel the movement and the stillness around me. So much activity, but it feels like all the same people taking part in the same activities. Perhaps it is the nature of the space, the people, or both pushing and pulling the other. Beyond Tan Man's spit take, there is no drama to be found in this garden. I start to get a little bored and thirsty. I decide to walk the half-mile back to civilization. I get a few meters away from the bench when I hear someone behind me say, "Hey, man."

They are likely not talking to me, as strangers rarely do, so I keep walking. A moment later I hear again, "Hey, man," and feel a tap on my left arm.

I turn to see a fellow standing before me holding a notebook that looks a lot like my notebook. It even has the same pen I have stuck in the spiral bind. I realize it is my notebook, given that I do not have mine in my hand. Also, the fellow is Hector.

Thank you, I say, reaching out for him to hand me the notebook.

"*No hay problema*, man," he says.

He looks at me. I look at him. I nod, thank him again, turn, and walk away.

I go no more than a few steps before turning around with a smile on my face. Hector laughs. Loudly. Loudly enough that some of the tourists nearby stop taking pictures and look over at us, annoyed at the disturbance. Where was their ire for Tan Man?

"Funny," says Hector.

One question, I prompt him.

"Okay...?"

What month is it, I ask.

"October. Why?"

I was not sure when now is, I answer.

Hector squints his eyes at me, trying to discern if I am joking around. I am not.

"Okay, yeah. October."

We stand there, facing each other, in an awkward moment of silence.

"Saw you sitting over there for a bit. Didn't know if you were interruptible, so I kinda hung back. Then I saw you left your notebook and figured I'd help," says Hector, breaking the silence.

I thank him again. He suggests that we sit on a nearby bench, but I shake my head no and tell him that I am entirely too warm and am in need of a cold beverage.

"Well, I was leaving, too. Mind if I walk with you," he asks.

I tell him I do not mind and we begin our trek back down the hill along the circuitous paths that connect this part of the park with the *Alphabet District*. We pass a fountain to collect some coolness off the spray and then stop for a moment at the *Sacajawea* statue.

"It's cool to stand where Eva Emery Dye once did," says Hector.

I nod as if I know who that is. Someone to look up at the library, I suppose. I read the commemoration aloud:

Erected by the women of the United States in memory of Sacajawea, the only woman in the Lewis & Clark expedition, and in honor of the pioneer mother of old Oregon.

We continue north and find our way along a path that empties out at Burnside and NW 24th Place. As we walk past *Twist*, I glance in to see if Cairene is working. I suspect she is in class all day, but look anyway. She is not there. Hector steers us down to 23rd, then up to Hoyt. We cross and I follow him down a few steps at the corner and into *The Ram's Head*.

I do not think I have ever been in a place with so many tasseled lampshades, I say, as the entirely-too-cold-by-comparison air greets us.

Hector keeps us moving through the space until he finds two chairs somewhat away from the crowd. It is very busy, but it does seem as if this spot will allow us to chat without raising our voices.

We sit and a server comes to offer water and take drink orders. Hector orders a beer. I pull a thinking-face with a long pause to see what her reaction is.

"What kind of beer do you like, hon," asks the server.

I like trying different kinds of drinks, I say.

This seems like a tactic that will allow me to fit in with what Hector is ordering without actually ordering alcohol myself. Smooth.

"Sure thing," she says and wanders off.

"Were you hitting on her," asks Hector.

I shake my head no.

"Oh. That 'whatever you like' part sounded like a line," he explains.

I let him in on my secret, which I am not generally keeping secret.

"Oh," Hector exclaims. "Ummm... well... I guess we'll roll with it."

Indeed we will, I say.

I am only a year away from being legally allowed to drink, though even when it is legal, I doubt I will go out of my way to do it. It was 6 years ago that I was offered my first alcoholic drink in a restaurant. I never ask, but always have looked old enough to be served.

My eyes wander around the room. It is packed with comfortable furniture, lamps, art, photographs, coffee- and end-tables. The room seems designed to keep you in your spot, drinking the night away. I doubt we will sit here long enough for it to get dark out.

The server brings our beers. "Here's your Hillsdale Ale," she says to Hector. "And for you, a Black Widow Porter. First batch ever."

She prompts us for food, but Hector waves her off.

I take a sip of mine and am immediately sure I do not like Porters. Hector takes a long pull of his and we continue to sit in silence. It feels awkward. Much like on the Shin, I force my brain to think of something polite and inquisitive to ask to get him talking. But this time, Hector beats me to it.

"First time up at the garden? You know, there's a lot more up there beyond the roses."

I nod. First time. Seemed like a good place to rest for a bit. I did not know there was more to it other than more trees, I say.

"Yeah, man, there's so much up there. I don't go up often, but there is a good view of Wy'east from the Japanese garden, assuming the weather is good."

I nod. Maybe I'll venture up there sometime, I say.

I take another sip of beer. It grows on me a little.

THANKS to Hector, I know that it is indeed October.

To me, October means cold, clouds, and snow. But it is hot here, with blue skies, green trees, and brown grass. I walk to the post office to mail a package to Molly—a thank-you for the plane ticket. There is no line and I mail the package quickly, then sense the need for caffeine.

Along the way to The Place, I stop at a travel agency in order to investigate the plane ticket prices to Europe. My time in Portland has been short, but I feel antsy to keep moving.

"Prices are very high right now. London is $760 and is Paris $930," says the agent, walking me through a few places I would like to go.

With the exception of Western Canada—because it is attached to Alaska—and 4 hours in Nogales, Mexico, I have never left the country. Which is part of what makes London, Paris, Lisbon, and Berlin so appealing. As starting points. Which makes me consider the possibility of flying one-way and staying as long as I can.

London is the least expensive on the list. I ask about a one-way ticket. The agent clacks away on their keyboard and I watch as the numbers paint slowly on the green-text screen.

Fifteen-hundred, I exclaim aloud, as I see the price display on the screen.

To which I receive a what-can-I-do-about-it shrug from the agent.

How can a one-way ticket be so much more than a round trip, I ask.

"I know. It seems like it should be half the price. Maybe a little more, but..." adds the agent with another shrug.

I imagine these foreign governments have a deal with the airlines. Keep one-way ticket prices high to discourage filthy Americans from staying too long. But I am an Alaskan, not an American, I yell, in my mind, at the imaginary immigration official. I get the sense that Alaska is seen as separate from the United States by the rest of the world—and they are not wrong.

To revive myself from the plane ticket sticker shock and the idea that my most ideal prospect for next steps is blocked, I wander back to The Place, narrowly avoiding be splattered by the City of Portland workers who are hydro-jetting pro-OCA graffiti off the sidewalk.

I walk in and am greeted with the The Place being somewhat in disarray. The tables along the wall are sitting in the middle of the room and a few people are hanging up new art. So, in addition to it being October, it must also be Thursday.

This new show is photographs. Again.

The previous artist used infrared film. Still life, landscapes, and a couple of portraits. Then used watercolors to liven-up the photos. One in particular was of a building that looked like a museum. It was a night shot and the only light available was from the street lamps along the road. The artist had slightly-yellowed the lamps and used a brilliant red on the steps leading up to the museum doors.

I wander the walls looking at the new art while I wait for my drink, currently being made by Andragon. This will be the fifth latte made by her and I am not looking forward to it, but no one else is working. Each interaction with her has been terse-to-rude from her side. In a way, the new show offers me the opportunity to not stand at the counter, waiting within glare-shot.

The new photographs are in vivid color, but they are lifeless. Nothing is left to the imagination. There are several shots at different angles of an old, beat-up Ford truck, of paint-stripped doors, and of the facades of run-down houses. The objects feel frozen in place by an uncaring photographer—trapped until the pictures are destroyed, and the unwilling subjects can get on with their lives.

I drink half of my Andragon-made latte and let the rest go cold as I read a book. After an hour, I decide to walk downtown. Down 21st, then a jog to Morrison, to 10th, and up from there to the *Portland State University* library. I go to look for information on college options—still thinking about going back to school even though, in many ways, it feels like that would be a step backward. This day has seen me in one building looking for options to roam the planet far and wide and in another building looking for options to plant myself in one spot for a while.

I have no idea what I should be doing.

I spend a few hours trying to figure out what I want to be when I grow up, while looking at endless lists of college requirements, tuition, and picturesque campuses. I find as much info as I can stomach—it is all too expensive—and decide it is time for lunch.

I walk around downtown in an aimless fashion. Along the park by the university, then a zig-zag back toward Cairene's neighborhood until I get to *Escape From New York Pizza*. It is a hole-in-the-wall joint with hand-thrown pizza and ice-cold root beer. I realize I end up here quite a bit in the time I have been here.

The Crazy Woman is here, as usual, but is on break. She is not actually crazy, but she is very friendly toward me, and that makes me uncomfortable. She likes to call me Smiley and does not seem interested in my actual name. The part that confuses me most is that she seems to have a genuine interest in me—which is crazy.

I get my two slices of pepperoni with black olive and a large root beer—

what I always order—and sit on a stool a few down from her. I shake a heap of fake Parmesan onto the slices and start eating. As soon as I have a mouthful of pizza, she asks how I am, how the writer's block is coming, and fits in a few other pleasantries that seem quite sincere while I stare back at her and chew.

I do not recall specifically what she asks, but as she pulls information out of me, I realize that I do not talk to people often. At some point into my second slice, a tiny voice in my brain says, tell her everything, and so I talk in what feels like excess. I tell her of ruts, of wandering, of feeling stuck again. She does not seem to mind.

It starts to get busy and she excuses herself to go back to work. I feel exhausted from sharing and full on pizza. I wish I could go back for a nap at Cairene's, but I am locked out for the next few hours. There are many places I can go, but somehow end up back at The Place.

Andragon is gone and The Necklace Man is in her place. The art is hung and there are a lot of people sitting at tables, but it is not as loud as in the morning—most of them are working on personal projects, like I should be doing. I ask The Necklace Man to make it a double. He smiles and pulls an Americano for me.

"No room for cream, I remember," he says.

The only table that is both open and not directly next to someone is in one of the windows that looks out into the street. I sit, place my cup on the right of the table, place my book on the left, and open my notebook in hopes I will write at least a few sentences. I am immediately saved by a, "Yo, man," from a familiar voice at the back of the room. It is Hector.

He sits at a table close to the stage. I look at him and back to my precisely set items. Out of habit, it feels like a toss up, but I side with being social as it means I can avoid the writing I need to do—and also I should practice being social.

I pack up and wander over. He moves his bag from the only chair available at his table and hangs it on the back of his. I nod and attempt as close to the same layout of my things as possible given I am now sharing a table. It is good enough for me to feel like I can write at any time, but I hope I will not have to.

"How goes, man," asks Hector.

I share the highlights of my life since our last meeting, of which there are few. I tell him about lunch with The Crazy Woman. He suggests I should start asking people their names instead of naming them. I shrug.

"People are more than the moment you meet them," he says.

Be that as it is, I agree, but also I would prefer not to, I say.

In the universe's perfect timing, The Necklace Man comes over with a drink for Hector. It looks like a caramel latte as there is a thick layer of caramel in the bottom of the glass and a long-handled spoon sticking out of it.

"Sorry it took so long. The caramel was in the fridge and I had to warm it up before it would come out of the bottle," he explains.

"No worries, man," replies Hector.

The Necklace Man wanders off to clear a few tables.

You know, I call him Man, too, I say.

"What," asks Hector.

You said man and I call him Man, too. The Necklace Man. See? You do not know his name either.

Hector stares at me blankly, then looks toward The Necklace Man.

"You know the difference, man," he says, emphasizing the word man. "Besides, his name is Michael."

I raise my eyebrows and attempt to portray mock incredulity.

Two Michaels. Good thing I call this one The Necklace Man, I say.

Hector shakes his head, rolling his eyes.

Okay. I know his name now, but I will likely continue to think of him as The Necklace Man. But I promise to not address him as such, I say.

Again, he shakes his head, rolling his eyes.

So...new art, I offer as a change of subject.

Hector leans back in his chair to look at the art closest to our table.

"Yeah," he says after a few minutes staring at the same piece, "I don't much care for it."

Me either, I agree.

I explain my thoughts about the previous show, which seems a decently apt comparison since they are both photo exhibits.

The previous show held a possibility of what might be, I say. I had wondered if the colors used by the artist were the real colors. I wondered what colors would I paint that world—what life would I give it.

"Don't get me started," says Hector, clearly wishing me to get him started.

Go on. Diatribe away, I say.

And he does.

"Good art demands interpretation. Requires it," he explains. "It is open to being questioned. It circulates and influences. Good art draws you into its world—makes you invest a part of yourself. It makes you ask, 'What do

I see that is different from the artist or the guy leaning over the table I am sitting at in order to see the detail of the photograph?'"

We both glance up at this point in his diatribe to stare at the man partially leaning over our table to look at the same photograph that we are looking at. He does not look at us and after a few moments walks to the next photograph, toward the front of the room.

Hector and I both shake our heads and roll our eyes. People.

You were bemoaning, I prompt.

He stirs the caramel into his latte while thinking.

"I dunno, man. I know there are a dozen artists for each cafe in this town, but sometimes I have to wonder about the people in the cafes who pick the artists. There's a lot of good art in this town. Not all of it can sit on a cafe wall, but there's got to be better than this."

He trails off, still stirring his latte, then finishes the thought.

"I mean, I can do better than this."

He stands, with his latte in-hand and walks up to the counter to talk with The Necklace Man.

I stare at the blank sheet of paper in front of me. I understand this feeling is shared by many, if not all creators, but blank pages, like blank canvases, scare the crap out of me. I stare and stare and stare, completely unsure as to what should go there. In my current stack of books is one titled *Writing Down the Bones*. It offers sane, rational, reasonable advice. Much like most of the writing advice I have read, it boils down to: Write a word, then another. Repeat until finished. I find advice that is both tongue-in-cheek and true to be the most annoying—extra annoying in that no one explains how to tell when something is finished.

I pick up my pen, uncap it, and smash the nib into the paper. It is a cheap ballpoint, so I know it can take it. Under no circumstances would I do that with my *Copic*. I scribble my frustration onto the page. It looks like the cloud of dust that follows *Pigpen* from *Peanuts* around. I make it bigger and bigger, my pen falling from the page a few times and marking up the table. I stop and marvel at what I have wrought.

"Nice...art," asks Hector. He has been standing there long enough to watch me scribble, apparently.

It is not art. It is a word, I say.

Hector leans over the table, mimicking the fellow who bothered our space before, and looks at the scribble.

"Uh. What word would that be," he asks.

I am not sure yet, I say.

Hector nods.

"Better this word on the wall than what's up there now."

I nod and tell him I agree.

Hector sets his cup on the table and rummages in the bag hanging on his chair. Out from it he pulls a folded up chess board. He holds it up in such a way that it is clear he is asking if I want to play. I shrug and remove my writing stuff from the table so that he can set it up. He finishes and spins the board so that I play white. Within a few moves he wins.

Do you play a lot, I ask.

"Not really. Some. Want to play again," he asks.

I nod and set up the board, spinning it so that he plays white this turn. Back and forth we go for about an hour each winning a game then losing a game. We seem to be evenly matched in that we both mostly know how to play. Over the hour, with increasing frequency, Hector looks at his watch.

On our ninth or tenth game, I ask him about it. He stares at the board sitting completely still—as still as the lifeless photographs on the wall. After what feels like hours, he looks at me and explains, sounding very reluctant to do so for as long as it takes to say it.

"I go to therapy once a week. Been doing it only a short while. Got my appointment coming up soon. S'why I'm over in northwest. And why you saw me at the garden last week."

Oh, okay. Definitely don't mean to pry, I say.

"All good, man. To tell the truth, I don't really like going. The therapist sits there waiting for me to talk. Won't say anything besides, 'Hello, Hector,' and 'Until next time, then,'" explains Hector.

That would really annoy me, I say.

"Yeah, I guess," says Hector.

He says it in a way that I infer to be a solid *no duh*.

"There's a chess board in her office," he explains. "Last visit, I sat there as usual, talking a little, not getting much of anything out of the therapist."

He picks up his coffee cup, inverts the saucer, and sets it back down with a barely audible *clink*.

"Once in a while she writes something down on her notepad. I got the idea about half way through the session. Took all my patience to wait for it. She said, 'Until next time, then.' I got up, put my jacket on, and moved Queen's pawn to D4. She didn't do anything, just looked at me and smiled weirdly, so I left."

This makes us both laugh. His opening move at the therapist's office is what he has played in almost every game of ours so far. I was making the same move, too, but had to come up with something different for the sake of variety and not losing quickly.

I wonder, but do not ask, why he goes to therapy. I figure he will tell me if he wants. Asking about it definitely feels like the antithesis of "All good, man." I am not sure if there is a way to tell if a person needs therapy, but I do not get the sense of it for Hector. He always has a smile on his face. He greets strangers. He is generally amiable to the people he meets— including me. This is the exact opposite of me, which might be why we get along. Although, I suppose if I did not think of therapy for him, I might suspect his exact opposite a prime candidate. Food for not thinking about.

Speaking of food, I say.

"Were we," asks Hector.

No. Not really, but segues are not really in my bailiwick, I say.

"Bailiwhatnow," asks Hector.

Dinner. Food. Eat. Ugh, I say, enunciating each word in my best fake Neanderthal impression.

"You weird. Food good," replies Hector. "But it will have to wait until after my session."

He suggests *Casa U-Betcha* which is barely a short walk away on 21st. I agree to his terms and as he packs to leave, I walk up to the counter to order more coffee and a cookie to tide me over until I meet up with him.

He walks by on his way out and says, "Catch you later, Michael." The Necklace Man turns and waves. "Bye, Hector!" I get a *See?* look from Hector as he pushes open the door and turns left to walk up Glisan.

Yes. I see. People have names.

The Necklace Man makes another excellent cup of coffee for me and I spend the next hour with my notebook open in front of me. I do not write a single word. Not even a scribble word or an art. I spend the time thinking about art and storytelling. Each time an idea comes to mind, I pick up my pen only to put it down again. I repeat the pattern. It starts out as a fun distraction, but quickly turns into something on the edge of obsessive. I know I am trying to keep myself from making a decision, but I am unsure what that decision is. I keep track of the clock and finally it is close enough to when I am supposed to meet Hector that I stop distracting myself, pack up, and walk over.

The outside of *Casa U-Betcha* is a very plain storefront. The inside is a rather cacophonous place. Music blares, people laugh and talk over the music. Hector is sitting at a table and waves me over. I greet him and get a "*Huh*" look from him as he cups his ear. I have no idea how we will have a conversation.

Hector orders the wild boar with what looks like a mole sauce. We ask about it, but can barely make out what the server says—which seems to give him some small amount of pleasure. The Portland service industry seems to thrive on counter-culture, less so on table-service-culture.

I go all out with a gigantic beef burrito. It is decent enough and fills the Neanderthal hole in my stomach. Given how difficult it is to hear each other we do not linger over the food. As I throw my fifth wave to the server to get his attention in order to pay, Hector stands up.

"I don't feel so well," he says, loud enough that I can hear him, as he passes me toward the restrooms in back.

He is there long enough for four more waves and for the server to finally bring the bill. I have enough cash to cover it, but not enough for much of a tip—which I both feel bad about and also not so much. Hector comes back with either sweat or water on his brow. He does not look well. He passes the table, barely acknowledging me, and I follow him out.

On the street, Hector tells me that he vomited. Something he ate tonight, or maybe earlier in the day.

"The mole sauce tasted a bit weird," he says. "I dunno, man. I'm gonna stumble home. See ya."

Do you want help, I ask.

"All good. I'll see you."

I watch Hector shamble away, north along 21st. He turns right, out of sight at Hoyt.

I do not see him until his therapy day the following week in the produce section at *Durst's*. He is placing what look like one thousand oranges into a small shopping basket. I walk up behind him and can tell he does not notice me.

Scurvy, I ask, louder than I need.

"What," yelps Hector, clearly startled.

Scurvy, I ask again.

He looks at me for a few seconds as though he does not recognize me, then breaks into a smile. He looks down at the basket filled with oranges next to his right leg.

"Heh, naw, man. Just having a craving. Definitely food poisoning last week though. Was down for four days." He reaches down to pick up the basket. "Though the only really rough day was the first one."

We walk through the store as I fill my basket with some basics. Hector seems comfortable with solely oranges. I realize it is not the day of, but the day after his therapy session and ask about it.

"Yeah, I went even though I didn't feel normal. Kinda have to. She did ask how I was feeling though. I guess I looked rough still. Kind of surprised me. It felt like I made contact with another life form, but after I said I was fine it went back to the usual stuff," explains Hector.

He tells me that the pawn is where he left it and that no other moves had been made. We check out, both at the same time, but in separate lanes, and meet outside.

"Well, time to ward off that scurvy I've been hearing about," says Hector.

He waves and walks away.

I stay away from The Place for a while for no particular reason I can point to. I spend most of my time wandering around downtown trying out different places to plop myself down for a few hours. None of them fit well. Although I still eat most of my dinners at *Escape From New York*. I sit upstairs when I am not talking to, or more typically, being talked at by The Crazy Woman.

I also spend a lot of time wandering around *Powell's Bookstore*. I like the Blue Room the best, though Purple and Green are good, too. Still no *Blue Highways* to be found. On one of my many days wandering different colored rooms, I find there is a cafe in the building. I am both surprised and not at all surprised that I never noticed—lots of books in the way.

I spend a few hours people-watching out the cafe window and leafing through books I will likely not buy. At some point the street lights come on and I realize it is late enough that Cairene is home and I can get inside.

As I walk in, I am greeted very warmly by her. We talk for a bit and decide to go out for dinner. It is First Thursday again and I am not sure how time keeps passing. First Thursday of course means gallery openings. We keep to walking distance from her apartment, though that still leaves us with over thirty galleries to choose from. The gallery closest to her place has a map of all the openings and each dot notes who is showing, what kind of art is there, and, most importantly, if there is free food and cheap booze available.

We wander from gallery to gallery with no real need for the map as most places we want to go are spilling out into the street with beautiful people, sometimes beautiful art, and always loud music which you can hear blocks away. It helps guide us through the darkened alleys that make up the industrial area that separates the northwest residences from downtown.

At several galleries, some of the Shares are backed up as the small crowds negotiate the space between having fun and allowing the autonomous vehicles to move through to where they are needed around the city. Generally, in each gallery, there is a fair bit of good art, mixed in with bad art, some strange art—to me—and all of it is overpriced. Well, more than I can afford. And there's also that pesky issue of having no walls of my own on which to hang said art.

I do understand that art supplies are expensive and creating art is time consuming. But as we look at some of the art, I have to wonder who would pay that much. At the fifth or sixth gallery we stop at, one piece catches my eye and really underscores that question of Why? It looks as though the artist took a tube of black paint and squeezed it all out onto the canvas, then let it dry. No brush strokes, just a line of paint moving around the canvas. There are no art patrons around this one sipping sparkling white wine while *hmm*-ing thoughtfully and nodding earnestly.

We spend four hours visiting roughly fifteen galleries and find fun art in about half of them. We have a good time overall. Free food and dollar booze certainly helps. Thoroughly full on appetizers and wine we stagger home.

The alcohol affects me more than I wish. As we take turns changing for bed in the bathroom, I have a difficult time keeping the floor from rising up and hitting me in the head. Cairene leaves the kitchen light on for me to find my way to the futon.

I pass by her Murphy bed, turn off the light, and use what remains of my mental faculties to keep myself from getting in bed with her. I do not want sex. I doubt I could handle any of the traditionally required movement anyway. What I want is to snuggle up with someone and drift off to sleep. I laugh out loud at myself as I lay on the futon hoping for the room to stop spinning, but also enjoying the ride.

Cairene mumbles something. I ask her to repeat herself, but she is fast asleep and I follow soon after.

I had a great time tonight, out amongst the people and with a good friend. And I feel lonely.

I wake what seems not long after with the sunrise. Birds call out, welcoming the sun. A lioness stands before me and rakes her claws through the air between us, protecting her territory. Her claws gleam in the morning light. Then, silence. My heart, beating so rapidly, comes to a stop. I stop breathing. Even the slight breeze rolling across the savanna ceases to caress my sweaty brow...

"I was wondering," says Cairene between sips of coffee, "while you are doing your thing today, would do me a favor?"

I sit up on the futon, still in couch-mode as bed-mode was too far out of reach for me last night. My head still stuffy from the gallery-hopping. There is something to the tone of her voice that makes me nervous about this favor she is asking for.

Of course, I say, timidly.

"I was wondering if you could start thinking about your next destination. I've been doing a lot more work at home than I had expected and I need my space back. I think it's time for you to go."

Sure, I assure her.

"Thanks. Let me know this weekend," she says, and stands to take her breakfast dishes into the kitchen.

I pick up a book and start to read. I am going to take this in stride. Or try to, but I can barely focus on the words in the book. My mind is going everywhere and nowhere at once. I know it is time to move on, I can feel it, but I am not ready to think about this. How am I going to decide this by the weekend? The weekend starts tomorrow.

Cairene leaves for work and I start to plan my day. I leave without a shower and go to the bookstore up the street in search of a road map of the western United States. They direct me to a tobacco shop a few blocks away on 23rd. Among the cheap novels, comic books, sex magazines, and stifling smell of moderate-quality tobacco, I find what I am looking for.

The day is turning quite hot—it has not rained the entire time I have been here—and I can already feel that it would be a more comfortable day had I taken a shower. I can barely make out the time and temperature sign above the bank a block away. It looks like it says twenty-eight Celsius. Which is ridiculous for ten in the morning, even in not-Alaska.

Perhaps coffee will help.

I go to a new cafe that opened last week across the street from Cairene's apartment building called *Ken's Artisan Bakery*. It smells wonderful, but I only have enough money for a cup. I order an americano and pick up the classified section from the local paper off the table next to me. Cairene said, "next destination," but another option enters into the what-the-hell-do-I-do-next pool of ideas as I sit down to wait for my drink to be made.

I could get an apartment of my own. In Portland. With walls for art. Perhaps even in this neighborhood. I scan the listings and my mind swims in and out of the what-the-hell pool. Why get a place here, I mumble to myself as I circle possibilities. Why did I leave home in the first place? To get out of Alaska and see things. I am supposed to be de-rutting. I do not want to be stuck in a particular spot.

If I stay here I will need a job. The easiest job for me to get is probably at a cafe. While it will likely be easy to get a job, and finding a place to live is easy enough, the problem lies with Cairene. Can I get her to let me stay through next week? I decide to go downtown to attempt to charm her. Or, more likely, get on my hands and knees and beg.

Along the way, I decide to check out yet another option. Down Morrison on this ridiculously-hotter-now autumn day, I slalom my way through the other people walking around the city. Everyone seems to be out today. My attention is drawn to a school bus driver squealing her bus to an abrupt stop.

"Look out, little girl," yells a passerby to a kid, no more than ten years-old, in the crosswalk. Luckily, she did look out.

I try to stay in the bits of welcome shade found beneath the tired, old buildings. I find the specific tired, old building I am looking for and walk in, then up six floors on a very fast elevator, to *Council Travel*. It is a travel agency that specializes in getting people like me to anywhere in the world as cheaply as possible.

I read brochures, glance around at enticing posters, and ask a great deal of questions to the woman behind the counter. I exhaust my questions relatively quickly—thank you, informative brochures—and feel eager to get out of there and back on the go. I leave with the knowledge that Europe is a stone's throw away and all at a relatively reasonable price, too. Assuming I do not mind taking six planes to get there and coming back to Portland once along the way for some reason.

I walk down another two blocks to where Cairene works. She is not in the store.

"In the food court," says one of her coworkers.

The unstoppable merchandising blitz reminds me why I hate malls—too much for my senses to take in all at once. The noise, the colors, so many people confined inside. I force myself to take a breath and wander into the food court—which adds smells to the sensory assault. I am unsure why it is so difficult to parse. I find Cairene and tell her my plans. To my amazement, she does not mind me staying an extra week while I figure out which path to take.

"You giving me a plan means I can plan for me," she explains. "I could tell you were thinking about it and really weren't sure of what to do. I figured you needed a kick in the ass, that's all."

I decide to try The Place again. As I walk in, I hear Meg's voice in the back of my mind yelling, "Rut!"

While I do like walking through this door, Meg's reminder prompts me to start thinking about finding a new place to be my new The Place. I hear "Rut!" again and begrudgingly nod my head as I walk in and *yeah, yeah, yeah* under my breath. Forget a new place. I should find a new city, but today I found a cheap-ish apartment up Glisan and figure I'll try on Portland at least until I get antsy or run out of money. Perhaps this city is the rut I am looking for.

Andragon waves me over to the far end of the counter to tell me I have a few messages waiting for me. Which is odd. It is odd that Andragon is being marginally pleasant to me and it is odd that I have messages. I do not have a phone and with as much time as I tend to spend here—even though I have not been in for a while—I suppose this is where people can find me. Which means I have been here long enough for people to want to look. Also odd.

There are four messages in total. Two of the messages are from Hector, one is from The Necklace Man asking me to work for him five days prior, and the last is from Andragon about how The Place is not my personal message board. I look up after reading the final message. There is a less pleasant smile on her face now.

The first message from Hector asks where I am. The second simply, "Queen's knight to C6."

Two more days pass before I see Hector. I walk into The Place with a book, writing gear, and a small grocery bag in tow. He sits in the back of the room at a table on the stage. A chess board is set up and there is a latte sitting on the table at the empty chair's spot. I walk up to the table, gain

Hector's attention, and tilt my head indicating the latte.

"I saw you walking down Glisan. Figured you were coming here," he explains.

I nod, reach into the *Durst's* grocery bag, and pull out an orange. I place it in front of Hector and then grab one for me as well. I sit and take a sip of my latte. It is not as hot as I would like and while it is a nice gesture from Hector to have it ready for me, lattes should be hot. Or cold. Never warm.

I set my orange on the table next to my cup and spin the board so that Hector plays white.

I take it by your note that she made a move on you, I ask.

Hector politely smiles at my terrible joke. "Yeah, she couldn't resist my charms any longer."

It seems like it is kind of silly paying so much money to play chess, I say.

"Nah, besides I'm not paying for it. My father is."

I stay quiet for a moment. He does not seem to mind my question, but he is not following up his explanation with anything but an opening move. As I ponder my opening move, I find that I am actually curious about it.

Why is your father paying, I ask.

I move my first piece and take a sip of an even-less-hot-now latte.

"He thinks I'm gay and wants the therapist to fix me," he answers, flatly, making his next move quickly.

I put my cup down and make my next move. It is difficult for me to tell how he feels about that. I am unsure whether to make a joke, be serious, or say nothing. Of the three choices, I feel as though I have to fight most against the many years of habit of cracking wise. And today, like most days, I lose the fight.

Well, that's one more thing we have in common, I say.

"What's that?"

We both like chess, lattes, and oranges. And everyone seems to think we're gay, I explain.

Hector stares at me. His eyes narrow, brow furrowing. There is otherwise no readable expression on his face. After a full minute of silence, he picks up one of my pawns and places his knight in its stead. I think to myself, perhaps habits of cracking wise, like ruts, need to be fought harder against.

The right corner of his mouth twitches.

Or not fought, I say, finishing my thought out loud.

I call his bluff and laugh loudly. He cannot hold it in any longer and laughs with me. The Place is somewhat busy and as our laughter subsides I notice everyone is looking at us with perturbed stares and it does not matter one bit.

The next few days pass with nothing of note happening and I am back to not keeping track of what day it is. I wander the general neighborhood, Hector and I play chess now and again, and I do favors for the people who work at The Place by picking up shifts for them so that they can enjoy glamorous nights out or whatever it is people get up to.

At some point during this time I remember to check my bank balance and feel glad there are some shifts to pick up. I likely should get a full-time job. Or move on, but I feel the pull of wanting everything to be familiar. I am getting used to the streets I walk. I am getting used to the people I see. I am getting used to working at The Place.

"Rut!"

I should move on, but familiar is familiar. Over and over, I find myself drawn back to The Place and tonight is no different. I sit at the counter, on a stool with one slightly shorter leg, rocking back and forth with a *clack* each time I move.

The bells which hang in the way of the front door chime and Myria scrambles in. She sits on a stool next to me and engages Andragon in conversation. They are going out on the town once Andragon finishes closing up and it must be nearing that time. There are still several people sitting at tables around the room, but there has not been a paying customer in for the entire time I have been here—including me as I work here often enough to get free drinks.

Myria is wearing...not even knee-high leather boots, almost waist-high. The definition of legs for days. She looks fantastic and it wrecks havoc with my hormones, which I find unnerving. We talk while Andragon starts the closing process in earnest, which includes scooting out the stragglers. She looks at me, not sure whether she should scoot me as well, but wanders away to remove dishes from the tables.

For the most part, I have trouble paying attention to what Myria is saying. I try, but it is less the befuddling of hormones and more the loud arguing with that part of my brain, telling it to pay attention to her. I keep track enough to stay mostly engaged, but sense she can tell the effect she is having on me. She excuses herself to use the restroom. I finish off the last of my coffee in a big gulp and my bladder immediately draws my full attention. I feel awkward having to go down the hall directly after Myria, but my bladder demands it and I wander back to the restroom.

As I finish up and come back out, Myria walks by toward the front. It feels like extremely awkward timing. Her long, brown hair swishes around her shoulders as she walks. She turns to look as she passes and has a warm smile on her face. I have no idea how to interpret it and am also unsure how to interpret my feelings and how to express them—or even if I should. I feel befuddled.

Back at the counter, I rip out a piece of paper from my notebook. I decide to vent the energy by writing a poem for her—straight through, no editing or thinking.

a miniature shower
wet hands
hair well groomed
I leave and see

long, brown hair
swishing along with the strut
a leather jacket
black not brown
I know a pirate that
be jealous of those boots

Her head turns to look
a brief smile from her red lips
I follow

I fold the paper and slide it to her.

Have fun tonight, I say, as I gather my things.

Myria pins the paper to the counter with her index finger and pulls it slowly toward her. I wave and turn to leave, nodding at Andragon on the way out. Once I am through the door and out of view, I begin to sprint. I jump over a couple of large garbage bags that are tossed in front of me by the flower vendor. I skip-step my way around people shuttling in and out of *Durst's*. Then I fly the rest of the way to my new place, just past the thrift store.

Iron gate, outer door, door to my studio apartment—I close each behind me and lean against the inside of my apartment door, nudging the deadbolt to locked with my elbow. I giggle in between heaping helpings of air.

I feel very young and stupid for writing a poem for her. Even more so for giving it to her. And it is a good, good feeling.

Hector and I spend the next evening playing chess at The Place. We are there until after closing and leave as Andragon finishes cleaning up. Hector invites me over to his place for more chess. And as the many cups of caffeinated beverages will keep me up for hours, I agree.

I find out that Hector does not live in Southeast as he said when we first met. He lives on the corner of 19th and Northwest Lovejoy, in the Royal Arms Apartments—which he tells me with the appropriate amount of fanfare and accent on Royal.

I wonder why he told me he lives where it is cheaper than in Northwest. I feel lucky to have found a place two blocks from The Place for only three hundred. I may have been able to find a cheaper place at the eastern edges of Portland, but I can do three hundred a month—for a couple of months.

He unlocks his apartment door and allows me to enter first. It is a studio, like mine, but almost twice as big. Again, why did he say he could not afford to live over here? Hector turns the overhead light on which reveals stacks of canvases everywhere there is space to put them. There are three easels each with two canvases on them.

Canvases rest against the back of the couch, several are in each of the three chairs around a table. On the table, under the table. There is a stack on the kitchen counter as well. I recall what he said on the Shin: "I tend to paint people who aren't people but also they are."

Is this cubist, I ask as I step around a stack leaning against the closet just inside the front door.

"I mean...yes," says Hector with an uplift at the end making it sound like he is unsure.

You have a lot of paintings here. Are they all yours, I ask. I stop counting when I get to forty—reminding myself I do not need to count everything—and have not covered even half of the room.

"Yeah," says Hector with a slight chuckle as he closes and locks the door behind us.

The canvas on the nearest easel is an exceptionally abstracted likely-person sitting on a likely-rock in a *The Thinker* pose. A larger one behind it is of likely-trees. Possibly.

How many are here, I ask, working my way around the couch to find a place to sit. Half of the couch and a chair by the window are the only two pieces of furniture here that do not have art sitting on them.

"Over a hundred, definitely," answers Hector.

My eyebrows elevate to become one with the ceiling. I look around and take the forty and roughly multiply by the space they take up and suspect the number is around one hundred and fifty.

I notice that there is no art hanging on the walls.

Hector finds his way to the fridge to get us a couple of beers. He hands one to me and sits across from me in the chair. He sets his beer down, picks up a chess board that is sitting on the floor next to his chair, and begins setting up the board for us to play.

I spend those few moments leafing through the stack of canvases next to where I sit on the couch. This stack seems to be all the same subject— some musical instrument, a clarinet or an oboe. Each one I leaf through seems to proceed to a new level of abstraction until the final canvas in the stack which is essentially a long rectangle using the same generally beige color palate of all the pieces that preceded it.

Okay, so, not Cubism, I ask.

"No, it definitely is. I just," he pauses, trying to think of the right word. He spins the board so that I am playing white. "I guess I just don't like labels too much. Most of the ones you can see would definitely be classified by others as Cubist. Not everything I paint is like that—some of it would be classified as Surrealism—but ... this is what's working for me right now."

I only guessed Cubism because everything looks so cubey, I say, as I make my opening move and take a sip of the beer.

Nice. Alaskan Amber. I'm from Alaska, I say.

"*Sí*. I know," says Hector.

I do not feel like I go on about it, but the way he says it makes me think I may mention it too much.

What is that a painting of, I ask, pointing to the third easel that is on the other side of his chair.

"I guess it would technically be Synthetic Cubism. What do you think the subject is," asks Hector.

I *umm* my way through another pull of beer while my brain tries desperately to come up with what all the shades-of-red boxes are on the canvas. Flowers, I ask, taking a stab in the dark.

Hector laughs, "Good eye, man. I gotta start being more obtuse. They are roses from the Rose Test Garden. I was sketching up there when I saw you."

I laugh, clearly not quite seeing roses specifically.

"It's what I like most about this style of art. You have to work for the answer. I want you to work for it. If you don't want to work for it, I'm not interested in your thoughts about it. Not, you-you, but general-you."

Yeah, I get that, I say.

"I don't specifically set out to be obtuse when I start a painting, but in a lot of ways, the thing I am creating is for one person. Sometimes it's me, sometimes it's someone else, but, generally, I have a single viewer in mind. If someone else gets it, great, but I'm not doing it for them."

By this point in our conversation, I have already lost the first match and see to setting up the board again. I spin it so that Hector plays white.

So, I begin to say, but Hector beats me to it.

"So... why don't I show things if I have so much that could be shown?"

I nod and take another sip of beer.

"I dunno, man. None of them feel finished, even though a good half of them probably are. I guess this is another aspect of me I'm not ready to be out there."

I like a lot of these. The ones I can see anyway, I offer as some level of encouragement.

"I'm glad. When I'm done with that one," he points at the one I identified with roses, "you can have it."

I shake my head. Absolutely not, I say.

"Why not," asks Hector as he watches me take yet another of his pawns.

Art should be purchased, not gifted, I say.

"Okay, you can buy it if I finish it. Cool?"

Yep, I can spare a dollar, I say, hiding my smile behind another sip of beer.

Hector takes one of my rooks by slapping it off the board with his knight. It falls to the floor and bounces onto the carpet, then on top of a stack of small canvases.

Oh, is it like that now, I ask.

"Oh, yeah," says Hector with mock aggression, then picks the rook up and places it gently on the table next to his side of the board.

We end up playing another few games of chess and talking about his painting and photography. It is well past two in the morning before I notice the time. I can barely keep my eyes open. Hector offers the couch to me and I accept. He takes some canvases off a stool and puts it in front of his chair, then lays back with his feet up and tries to get comfortable in his chair. We try to sleep, but the night is extremely humid and still quite warm, which makes for an uncomfortable attempt at it—this city never seems to cool down.

Hector has no air conditioner and we spend the better part of an hour tossing and turning to get comfortable. I then hear a noise from the apartment next door and look at the clock on the wall. It is exactly three in the morning. I hear the voice of a woman through the wall. She is talking, but sounds agitated. I cannot understand what she is saying, but she stops talking at the same time I hear a heavy clump sound—which my to my imagination sounds like a body hitting the floor.

I sit up and look over at Hector. He faces the shared wall of the two apartments and his eyes are wide open. We can hear a man's voice now, speaking in Russian, I think. Then the woman's voice again, and I can hear her well enough to guess she said thirty dollars. Hector sits up and shrugs at me. I shrug back.

Our heads swivel back to the shared wall as something solid hits against it from the other side. Then another. There is some quiet talking, then another thud. And again. And again. It starts in spurts but eventually finds a rhythm that cannot be anything else than the head board of the bed hitting the wall.

Hector and I look back at each other, then at the wall again. The semi-rhythmic thud continues. We fall back on our respective sleeping spots, but face each other from across the room. The sound continues for a few minutes and we are treated to a cry of release from a single voice. It is not the woman. After a few minutes, we can hear quiet talking again, then footsteps, a door closing, and then footsteps passing on the other side of Hector's door on the way out of the building.

Neither of us can sleep and so we sit there, with barely a breeze coming through the open windows, and talk quietly about nothing in particular—nothing I can recall at least. It is almost four in the morning when we hear footsteps in the hall, possibly more than one person. Another door closing. Some quiet talking. The still stiflingly humid air is silent for a few seconds as Hector and I hold our breaths, waiting for something to happen.

The wall then begins to beat a steady tattoo, interspersed by the heavy groaning of a man and the half-hearted encouraging cries of a woman. Hector and I look at each other and both laugh out loud at what we are hearing.

Hector goes into the bathroom. I laugh to myself as the sounds from next door continue. Hector stops by the fridge on his way back and brings two beers with him. He hands me one and we drank them quietly, me on my couch, him sitting in the middle of the floor next to the table with the in Portland. There are a few small tables to either side. In between each table it is wooden storage crate. A deli case is lit up as the main attraction, roughly in the middle of the room, though it is empty.

"We're finally expanding," says Michael.

Cool. What are you going to do with it, I ask.

"Takeaway deli food mostly. And pizza."

Ah, I say.

I vaguely recall my conversation with him, possibly many weeks ago? What is time? I step up to the deli case and look around behind it. There is a metal platform with a concrete disc resting on top of it. I guess it to be about 2 meters wide.

What is that for, I ask.

"The pizza," says Michael.

I look again and then back at Michael.

"We need to build it. On top of that platform. And, actually, I was wondering if that was something you can do."

From scratch, I ask, tilting my head to one side.

Michael laughs. "No. We have an oven that we bought from a place in Italy. Each piece is in the crates." He points around the room at each crate. There are six of them.

Are there directions, I ask.

"Yep."

He reaches up on top of the deli case and hands me a manual. Which is written in Italian. I flip through it and see there are instructional illustrations for how to put it together. It all seems relatively straightforward.

chess board. He slowly spins the black queen between his fingers.

The sounds stop for no more than a minute then began again, this time with a little less vigor. As that is happening, we hear a door close and then again footsteps passing Hector's door, leaving the building. The groaning and grunting continue. Hector and I look again at each other with eyebrows raised and the sounds from next door stop.

I feel irritated, tired, and amused. We finish our drinks. Hector lays back on his chair and we settle in for another attempt at sleep. Within five minutes, the head board begins to pound away at the wall. This time there was no sound of a closing door and footsteps outside. Hector stands and pounds on the shared wall.

"¡Hazlo en silencio!"

The head board comes to a halt and we hear the muffled voice of the woman say, "Soh-ry," as the beat begins again with less intensity.

The depressant part of the second beer kicks in. Neither of us can stay awake much longer. Eventually, we drift off to sleep to the muffled sounds of a woman and some undetermined number of men trading money for sex.

After roughly five hours of sleep on Hector's uncomfortable couch— which I find out upon leaving is a bed, but he doesn't have room to open it due to the canvases—I make my way to The Place to help wake myself up. I get my usuals and make myself stay in order to write. Within minutes, Michael—the owner one, not the necklace one—interrupts my writing-not-actually-writing time to invite me to come next door with him.

We leave The Place, turn left and immediately enter the small space next door which has been shuttered for at least as long as I have been

It seems relatively straightforward, I say.

"Perfect. I gave a leaf-through of the manual and got what we need to hold each piece together. You'll have to mix it and trowel it in. And," he pauses with a slight wince, "I need it done by Sunday."

What day is today, I ask.

He looks at me as if puzzled by my question. "It's Thursday. I want to do the first firing on Sunday. Monday at the latest."

Okay. Regular rates apply, I ask.

"Yep. Regular pay and coffee. And pizza when it's done."

Can do, I say.

Michael leaves me to it. I leaf through the manual more slowly, picking up what very little Italian I can translate, plus some borrowed words. The illustrations are the usual mix of helpful and confusing for things like this. Within minutes I have to track Michael down for some basic tools to open the crates.

Inside the first crate is a lot of straw. I begin to remove it and see a terracotta triangle poking out. The straw is immediately itchy and smells very musty. I grab some dish washing gloves to avoid the sensation as much as possible. Once most of the straw is out, and strewn around floor, I hear footsteps behind me. I turn to see The Necklace Man peering easily over my shoulder and looking in the crate.

"It looks like an orange slice," he says.

I agree with him and explain that each slice will come together to form the dome of the oven.

"Yes, I got that already. I know what a pizza oven looks like," he says.

Fair, I say.

I push some of the straw out of the way of my feet. I try to lift the wedge out of the crate, but it is too heavy and awkward.

"That part's why I am here," says The Necklace Man.

He is tall and his broad shoulders are accentuated by his iconic denim overalls—I have rarely seen him in anything else. For as much space as he takes up physically, he seems to take up the inverse amount with his demeanor. The Necklace Man is a calm, quiet, and kind fellow.

He suggests lifting the crate onto the table next to it and we do so. We use a hammer and a small crowbar to open the side, then slide the wedge out at hip-height.

Much easier, I say.

"Brains and brawn," replies The Necklace Man with a broad, warm smile.

We take the wedge to the platform behind the deli case and lay it on its edge to reduce the likelihood it will crack. Over the next hour, we repeat the process with the rest of the crates, leaving the final piece safely in its crate to address combining the pieces that are already on the platform into their dome shape.

Each wedge has a tongue on one side and a groove on the other. It takes some effort—and we wrangle Shane to help. He is one of the other very-part-time employees at The Place. Eventually we get the pieces to stand on their own, minus the one still in its crate.

I let them both wander off as the next step is to apply heat-resistant grout to the seams on the inside of the dome. It is easy enough to climb onto the platform and squeeze through the spot where the final wedge will go. I set about applying the grout, crouched down in the middle of the platform.

After making my way through two seams, I hear the front door open, thanks to the voices flowing in of people walking along the south side of Glisan. I figure it must be Michael, but then comes an "Excuse me," from a voice I do not recognize. At least, it is not a voice I recognize to be in Portland.

I try to stand without bumping any of the wedges and my knees protest at the effort. I feel like I am not supposed to have knee problems this early in life, but my knees have been this way for a decade. With a grunt of effort, I pop up from within the almost-finished pizza oven and see that on the other side of the deli case stands Orla.

Orla does not belong in Portland. She is an Anchorage person. Yet, here she stands. She is looking in the deli case and around the room. It looks as though it is slowly dawning on her that this is not a place that is open. I do not feel like having Anchorage and Portland too close together, so I clear my throat to get her attention and tell her that this part is not open, but she can go next door for coffee and pastries.

She looks directly at me as if startled. Which makes sense—from her point of view, she was in an empty-of-people room. She spins in a circle as if unsure of her surroundings and wobbles a bit. Is she drunk, I think to myself.

"Hey," she yells with a broadening smile.

Yes, it is me, I say.

And that is enough to open the fire hose of everything that has transpired over the time between the last time we saw each other in Fairbanks and now.

She tells me about her new dog, a pit bull, and how it attacks everyone in sight. "Isn't that great," she asks. Then on to how she is reading Dostoevsky. "Every time I read *Brothers Karamazov* I love it! I don't think I'll ever get tired of it." Her words lilt and slur. She is decidedly drunk. I try to point her toward the coffee next door. She waves me off and tells me how she is teaching little kids to "really think" before their minds are turned to mush by the establishment. "Do you have any free time," she asks, adding "Here's my number," and then gives me directions to her house instead—which sounds as though it is in Southeast. Then an invitation to drinks at a place by her house. "By the way, do you know..." Six or seven people are listed and I do not know any of them. Strip ping-pong and people in their underwear. "Surely you heard about it?" She seems to have no clue that our lives are so drastically different, but she must tell me everything that she is doing. It confuses me that she wants to share any of this with me. The dog again. "Come see it, I tied it up outside...gained so much weight... pulls me down the street. I fly!" She does not take the hint when I mime being unable to find a pen for her to write her number down. When I relent and offer her my Copic—always in my right front pocket— she puts it in her mouth while trying to remember her new number. "Did I show you my latest tattoo," she asks, handing my pen and the paper with her number to me—paper she ripped off the instructions for building the pizza oven. The part of the instructions I am on right now. I remind her that we have not seen each other for a long time, though as I say it, I wonder if it is true. "Right, right. But let me show you," she exclaims with a big smile on her face. She is wearing denim overalls with the legs cut off just above the knee. She unhooks the first strap as she turns to face away from me. As she reaches to undo the second strap, Michael walks through the front door carrying a large paper bag with both hands. She unhooks the second strap and the overalls fall to the floor. She twists to point to the tattoo on the lowest part of her back. She is not wearing any underwear. Michael stops in his tracks, staring, I assume from the angle, at her not-covered-with-underwear crotch. "Amazing, right" asks Orla, twisting more to look at me. Very, I say, with my eyes well-averted. I am not sure what it is a tattoo of, as I turned my head before being able to see it for more than a blob of black ink. She smiles, then turns to face forward, bends over to pull up the overalls, and begins refastening the straps. Michael remains fixed in place. I look at him and grab his attention with a wave and a give-me-a-moment hand gesture. Orla is oblivious to him as he passes behind the deli case and into the storage room behind where the pizza oven sits. After all this, she looks up at me—I am still standing inside the partially put together pizza oven—and asks, "So what are you up to these days?"

HECTOR and I sit on the patio at *Lechon* waiting for our food to arrive.

It is almost nine at night, which suits me as I prefer eating late. Hector sips his beer, a dark ale from Henry's brewed only a half mile away. I drink water. I do not feel like having alcohol tonight given how little and how poorly I slept at Hector's last night. Perhaps was it last week...

The night air has a surprising bite of autumn crispness to it, but it was a hot enough day that we are both comfortable sitting outside. The sun has been down a few hours and the waning gibbous moon is low on the horizon coming just off of full two nights ago.

The patio is crowded with couples and groups enjoying each other's company. Hector stares at the moon, not speaking. He gets like this sometimes and I do not mind at all. It is good to sit quietly and share a view with someone. Hector sets his glass on the table, hitting his fork along the way for a loud *clink*. I look at him with mock horror that he ruined the silence.

"You know, *ese*, tha's where we came from."

There is a mild slur to his words as he points up at the moon.

I look at the moon, then obliquely, skeptically even, back at him.

"S'true," he assures me.

This should be good, I say.

I incline my head, letting him know I am ready to be regaled.

"About a million years ago, give or take," he begins.

Naturally...give or take, I say.

"*Héctor levanta la mano, ordenando silencio,*" he says, holding up his hand as if to command silence.

If Spanish is slipping out, I think to myself, the beer must be lowering the wall between his split lives. With extra emphasis so that I am sure he can see, I roll my eyes.

He is going to start over again, I say, so that he can easily hear me.

"About a million years ago, give or take, we lived on the moon. Not humans like we are now, but the way we were before we mixed with the beings of Earth."

He goes on to describe how our ancestors built great technologies, cities, and cultures, but then exhausted the resources of their small planet. Everything was dying and the Moon people decided to leave for Earth.

"They'd traveled here before the big migration, of course, but didn't do much more than some scientific study. Their home was the moon. They sat in restaurants, on patios, and gazed upon the Earth as we gaze on the moon tonight."

Hector tells me how the Moon people who came to Earth all agreed they would not let technology dominate them again. It was their obsession with convenience that did them in.

"Things were good for the Moon people for thousands and thousands of years. They lost their advanced way of viewing a planet, one which destroyed their former home, and thrived, though with hardship, to be sure."

Hector raises his voice. He's alternating sipping and gulping his beer as he tells the story.

"And they earned their place here, *ese*. Until one day, some dude was sitting there trying to break apart a cracked stone and thought, in his own way of thinking, 'This would be a lot easier if I had a long stick with a sharp or heavy rock tied to the end. I think the old ones called it a Hammer.'"

Our food arrives. Peruvian Roasted Chicken for me and the Nikkei-style Kalbi for Hector. The server asks if we want more of our respective drinks. I nod my head.

Hector hands the server his empty glass, says, *"Ein mas biru, s'il vous plaît,"* and continues his diatribe.

"And that hammer sealed our fate. Yours. Mine. Everyone on this patio. Some dude, thousands of years ago, couldn't be bothered to go find another rock. No. He wanted that rock. And that's all it's been since. Someone wants this rock or that rock, they get super specific about it. And for what? We live on a giant ball of rocks! Plenty to go around! But some idiot wants a specific rock. So he gets a hammer. And if someone else also wants the rock, well, *no hay problema*. He's got this fucking hammer."

"Technology, *ese*," he pauses to sip some of his newly arrived beer.

"Some of this shit is good, I'll grant you. I love this food, and so much technology was created to put it in front of me in just this way at just this time. But I didn't fucking earn this food. I did some activity using convenient things. Someone else thanked me for making things convenient for them and used a convenient thing, money, to thank me. So that I could sit with you on this patio and look up at that moon where we used to live and marvel at how good we have it here. I didn't earn this food. But I get to pretend I did because that fucking guy made a fucking hammer. Fuck technology."

Fuck it, indeed. But I am going to eat this food now, I say.

"Hell yes. Smells so good."

We dig in. It tastes as good as it smells and looks. The moon rises above us, losing its yellow color, passing far enough above the horizon to turn blue-white. We fall again to silence, watching the moon ascend and eating excellent food.

I sit back in my chair between bites, with my glass of water in my hand, and I think about the silliness of Hector's story. And I think about what it must be like to really earn something.

A couple hours later, Hector and I meander our way back to our general neighborhood. It is quite chilly now which is such a welcome change in weather and I hope it lasts. We run into Susan as she steps out of The Place after closing. Susan started full-time this week and it makes me wonder what it takes to get full-time work in this city. Probably trying to get full-time work would have an impact.

Hector and I wanted coffee after our luxurious dinner, but missed it by at least a half hour. She invites us over to her place as she is wired on coffee herself—lucky her—and we both have nothing better to do.

Susan's apartment is an old house on Pettygrove, between 23rd and 24th, that has been divvied into three apartments. We wander in to find a small, but tidy one-bedroom. The only mess, if it can be called that, is two pizza boxes neatly stacked on the coffee table. Everything else is meticulously set in its place.

I wander through the living room, through the open French doors, to stand on the Juliet balcony. I look up and down Pettygrove. The street is quiet except for the breeze that rustles some of the remaining leaves on the trees that line the streets. Under the street light in front of the house, a very old, brown Mercedes is parked and it blends in under the pile of leaves that encloses it. It is obvious that its owner has not moved the car in quite some time and it surprises me to see an actual car in the city limits.

On my way through the living room, I noticed a camera hanging by its strap on the wall next to the doors to the balcony. I grab it and take an overhead shot of the pile of leaves with the Mercedes inside. There is easily enough ambient light from the city that the exposure does not have to be very long. I think to myself, this could be on a cafe wall.

I hear the glass doors close behind me and turn to see Susan looking at me but also past me. Her red lipstick and red nails stand in stark contrast to her jet-black hair and alabaster skin—which I suspect is the point. She holds a wrinkled and torn piece of paper against the window and looks off into the distance. I raise the camera and capture the moment she wants to share.

The paper is a credit card payment receipt with Madonna's signature on it. *The* Madonna. Susan fades away from the frame of the glass door to be replaced by Hector. He holds up a pizza box, much the same way Susan held the receipt. Apparently it is time for more food.

A slice of *Escape From New York* in hand, we sit down to watch *The Adventures of Buckaroo Banzai Across the 8th Dimension*. Hector stretches out on the floor, a pillow propping up his head so he can see the TV. Susan and I are on the couch, at opposite ends. We are mostly quiet, pausing the tape now and again to grab a drink or go to the bathroom.

There are four guitars in a stand to the left of the TV. Susan is in a band called *The Four Jills*. She has an unplugged electric guitar in hand and is practicing scales quietly while we watch the scene in the movie where Buckaroo meets Penny Pretty.

"Is someone out there not having a good time," asks Buckaroo.

I am having a good time, I think to myself.

The scene finishes with Buckaroo's obtuse insight: "No matter where you go...there you are."

"Yeah," says Hector. I look over at him, expecting possibly another diatribe. His eyes are closed, but he seems to be listening to the movie.

I look at Susan. She is not watching the movie or listening to it, having moved on from scales to practicing a song. Eventually, the credits start to roll. Susan stands and turns off the TV and VCR.

"I'm tired," she says. She puts her guitar on the rack with the others and walks into her bedroom, closing the door behind her.

Hector and I have a shared moment of, *Well, okay then*.

We put the pizza boxes in the kitchen and tidy up. We leave without being able to lock the door, but neither of us wants to disturb Susan. I close the door more forcefully than needed to send her the signal we have left. She can lock it if she wants.

Hector and I walk our separate ways at the corner of 23rd and NW Pettygrove. He says nothing and only offers a grunt to my goodbye. I arrive back at my apartment and flop on my sleeping bag in the middle of the room. Still no furniture.

This is the second night in a row where I am awake well into the wee hours of the morning—though here I'll only be bothered if someone comes in the side door as my apartment looks out on that entry. I cajole my brain on the path to sleep, but eventually fall back on my trick of telling myself a story.

I think about a time in high school when we were late getting back after lunch. I sat in the back seat, in the middle with...and here my poor memory fails me as I cannot recall who is sitting next to me. But I do know Gordon was driving and Debbie was in the front passenger seat. The sun visor was down and she had the mirror open. She was putting on mascara, having spent most of the ride back reapplying her makeup. As we turned onto the dirt road that runs parallel to the school grounds, I encouraged warp speed from Gordon and he floored it. The tires of his Subaru spun, then caught traction, as we sped forward along the road. The turn-in for the parking lot arrived much sooner than Gordon was used to as he normally did not drive along this road so fast. He slammed the brake and we began to slide, the back end of the car trying to take the lead. Gordon whipped the steering wheel to the right and the momentum from the back of the car switched sides and again tried to precede us. We fishtailed past the entry to the parking lot and finally came to a stop, perpendicular to the road, except the last of the momentum still wanted to keep going and we tipped up on two wheels. Someone yelled, "Lean," and we all leaned the opposite direction, trying to keep the car from rolling. It slammed back down and a cloud of dust surrounded us to then be blown away by the wind. My hands were on either shoulder of the front seats. Gordon held his hands away from the wheel as if to say, "I'm not touching that anymore." It got very quiet, relative to how we arrived in this spot, and then a loud *snap* brought our attention to Debbie. She had closed the visor and the mirror's cover made the snapping sound. She turned to look at us and her makeup was perfect. All that, almost rolling the car, and her makeup was perfect. She smiled and said, "I'll get out here. Got class." Yes you do, I thought to myself, as she walked away from us as we continued to sit in the middle of the road and were starting to block traffic.

When I wake the next morning, I find I am smiling. Telling myself a story to fall asleep worked well and I think the memory I used put me in a good mood. It does not always work, given the poor state of my memory, but once in a while, when I really need it, this method helps soothe my mind and interrupts the loops of thoughts which build up sometimes.

I put myself together, not as elaborately or effortlessly as Debbie, and wander off to greet the day. I notice some color through the slot in my mailbox on the way out. I rarely think to look, but today I take out a letter from Sherry which I will read. After coffee.

I walk to The Place because the coffee is good and free. Mostly because it is free. I am beginning to suspect I am running out of money. I work only sparsely at The Place and Michael has no more pizza ovens for me to build. Though I am okay with that part. Building the final part of that thing had me crawling through the small arch that serves as the opening to the oven and applying the grout once in was challenging and claustrophobia-inducing.

I walk in and see Howie in front of me at the counter. I love Howie or, at the very least, I love the idea of him. He is a big man. Both in height and girth. He comes into The Place on a semi-regular basis. Beyond the bigness, his marking physical characteristic is his rainbow suspenders. At this point in his weight, he no longer buttons his pants, so the suspenders are not solely for show, even though they are clean and bright. One side or the other of his suspenders always seem to be twisted. Andragon often helps him straighten them out.

He sports a beard now. Could be an onset-of-winter thing, which I understand completely, even though the cold weather is not yet here—if it will even come. Similar to The Necklace Man, as much space Howie takes up physically, the space he takes up verbally is inversely proportional. He is a quiet man—barely says much. His hands shake, almost uncontrollably, unless he is holding something. Put a cup of coffee in his hand and he is steady as a rock.

Howie reacts to the world slowly and gently. He is hard of hearing. He loves to read each and every page of the paper, sometimes a few different papers, though it takes him a while. He plays chess and checkers with anyone that will join him. He takes his coffee with cream.

Howie is, what some might be inclined to call, a Local Character. Which, if you dwell on it too much, will take away from the charm of him. He seems depressed, but if you watch awhile, you'll see that he is slowly ingesting all that is before him and applying his understanding to the world. I am often afraid he is going to keel over from a heart attack or stroke. This is due mostly to his weight. I am afraid of him sometimes too. Partly because he is quiet, but mostly because he shakes.

When he goes, I suspect he will be missed by many people. And then, I think we will forget about him after a while. I hope not. He is one of those people that I will never be friends with and do not speak with much, except to occasionally serve him coffee, but I am nonetheless enamored with his existence. In a way, Howie reminds me of a low-energy Floyd.

I think of his similarity to Floyd because the letter from Sherry came with a newspaper clipping from the *Anchorage Daily News*.

"Wednesday morning, one of his caregivers found Floyd Kaleak dead, still seated in front of his television in the tidy white house he rented off East Third Avenue and Eagle Street. Kaleak, 45, appeared to have died of natural causes, Anchorage police said."

Growing up, I would see Floyd all over Anchorage. I talked with him once, briefly, earlier this year and well before Meg kicked me out of the state. He often stood at the southwest corner of Minnesota and Spenard, with a different sign each time, bouncing, smiling, and waving to the cars speeding by. I saw him standing in front of *The Kobuk*, hat in hand, showing police officers his business license to bring joy to others—and to receive payment for such—which is decidedly not panhandling.

My first reaction to Floyd was as a preteen—ignorant child quietly makes fun of unfortunate person with friends. Floyd scared me. Once I was in an environment that required I take responsibility for my thoughts and actions—I went to a weird high school—my view on Floyd changed. I did not understand him, but I accepted him without pity, fear, or mocking. He was Floyd and seeing him made me smile.

During this time Outside, I have come to understand there are not many Floyds in the world. There are wavers, smilers, followers, and panhandlers—with expectations and without—but, for the most part, there is nothing unique about them. They are a part of the city, but mostly they are cogs; a part of the machinery that moves a city and is moved by it. If one cog brakes down, there are others to take its place.

Floyd was not a cog. He was an important and necessary part of the machinery of the city: the oil. Floyd kept the city moving. He kept it from breaking down.

Commerce keeps most people fed and sheltered. Garbage services keep the land clean-ish. Traffic lights keep people moving, mostly, and not crashing into each other, mostly. While all these things that make a city function are important, they do not make it function well—only adequately.

Being involved in the commerce of a city usually allows you to pay for the most basic of life needs. A service that takes away garbage from living areas is an important factor to a healthy life. Traffic, still very much a thing in Anchorage, allows you to get where you need to be—even when it is slow or seemingly unmoving. But once you have the basics taken care of, you yearn for more. Even if you spend all your time and energy making sure the basics are going to be there, you still yearn for more.

Floyd was that more. A smile, a wave, an expression of excitement about being alive. He was a human being who reached out every day, regardless of the weather. And even though most did not reach back, for whatever reason, he was there again the next day. I think about the vulnerability and strength it takes to be that for others. For Floyd, reaching out was a basic necessity that trumped those life needs to which the rest of us apply so much importance.

I saw Floyd move coins from people's pockets to his panhandler's hat. I watch Howie move chess pieces from one side of the board to the other. But those are side effects of the true impact: they move people.

It is easy enough to look upon the Floyds and Howies of the world as unfortunate people. It is also easy enough to flip that and realize they are out there, making the effort. Perhaps the world would actually be a better place if we could all be Floyd and make someone's day better by waving at them. Or be Howie and make someone's day better by giving them your undivided time and attention, if only for a little while. I think about the vulnerability and strength that must take and wonder how something simple can be difficult—I wonder why I struggle so much with it.

"What are you doing tonight," asks Hector, pulling me back into the room.

I find that while I have been staring at Howie, I have crumpled the news clipping in my hand. I look at Hector and wonder how I did not see him there. His voice seems overly loud. Was he having difficulty getting my attention?

Same as every night. Not a damn thing, I say.

"Incorrect. Tonight we're going to Albina Town for dinner and dancing."

That sounds fifty-percent appealing, I say.

"Incorrect. It is one hundred-percent appealing."

I am in, but remain one hundred-percent incredulous, I say.

"Perfect," says Hector.

He then turns and leaves as suddenly as he seemed to arrive. I watch him walk out. The Necklace Man waves to get my attention and tilts his head toward the front door with a quizzical look on his face. I shrug in answer. After staring at the front door wondering about Hector, I pack up my things and leave.

I spend the day mostly in my apartment tidying up what little there is.

I wash and dry all my laundry. I put my clothing in neat piles along the wall as I have no dresser to put them in. I clean the kitchen. I put away my sleeping bag even though I never do that. I take down the shower curtain and pick up the bathmat to wash them as well.

The bathmat does not come up easily. Somehow it is sticking to the floor. This moment pushes my ability to handle dirty things. On the plus side, I learn that bathmats need to be cleaned on a more regular basis. I decide to throw away the bathmat. It is entirely, in the parlance of the kids these days, too fucking gross to think about taking down to the laundry. How long have I been here?

The rest of the day moves along quickly. I spend a little time actually reading instead my typical starting at the pages and reading the same sentence eleventy times. Around four in the afternoon, Hector buzzes my intercom. I hear a "Let's go, yo," through the fritzy speaker.

I lock up and meet him out front.

Why so early, I ask.

"We're walking over. I don't want to take Public or Share tonight. 'sides, man, you need to move more," he says as he pats my gut.

I concede the fact with a begrudging grunt.

We walk down Glisan, past The Place, Cairene's place, the synagogue— with still-dripping spray-painted OCA propaganda on its red brick wall— and the theatre. Hector is silent most of the way except for a "Let's go," urging us to hurry across 16th before the light changes and we are further delayed by the sea of bicyclists heading home after work.

We walk through the station under *Stadium Gardens Park*. People are hurrying to catch the train out to the suburbs. Many people are in line for the *Sando and Sake* food cart. The line is long enough that it blocks the way to leave the station onto 15th. We push our way through, politely, and I grumble about peoples' ability to queue or lack thereof. Hector remains silent.

What is on your mind today, Hector, I ask as we pass *Andina*.

"Hm?"

Your mind, I repeat.

"Ah, nothin', man. Just bugged a little. Something's been buggin' me for a while and I can't shake it. No idea what it is. Not a big deal though. Guess I'm just lost in thought."

Cool, I say, feeling unconvinced, but I let it go.

My question seems to pull him out of his reverie and as we pass *Blick* he says, "Tomorrow, let's come back here and get some art supplies."

What kind, I ask.

"Doesn't matter, man. Let's just make some art together or something."

We continue walking down Glisan and, for several blocks, Hector provides some balance to the amount of silence earlier. He talks about how he has put his painting on hold. His father is an artist and he feels both a pull toward art and a repulsion. He dances around the topic of his father enough to tell me something has changed recently, but I do not push.

My mother runs the library system for the entire municipality of Anchorage, I say.

"What's a municipality," asks Hector.

I'm not sure exactly. Perhaps, it means loose governmental conglomeration of people who agree they basically live in the same place even though everyone is spread out over eleven-thousand miles because Alaska, I offer as explanation.

"How does your mom being a librarian fit with how my dad is an arti..." He trails off. "Yeah, I get it."

I hate reading. I will, and do, but I just don't enjoy it. Piles of books everywhere in the house and my mother reading instead of interacting. There is likely a lot to unpack there, but for the purposes of this part of our conversation, I hear you, I explain.

Hector nods. "How 'bout this: I do art, you do book."

Deal, I say. And I mean it.

I ask about his visits to his parents in Seattle in order to keep him talking. Which, for a moment seems to have the opposite effect, but then he states, "Just my dad" in a way that conveys his mother isn't around anymore. And then he surprises me by talking about his father more.

"He was a hippie when he was my age, but he is different now," says Hector.

A hippie, I ask.

"He met my mom in DC. They went there to levitate the Pentagon."

Did they, I ask.

"Inconclusive," he answers, with a slight, inward smile.

I am reasonably sure that is a *Simpsons* quote, but I let him continue rather than stopping to congratulate him on a superb reference.

"I came in to their story around ten months later. Apparently I traveled with them as they wandered, looking for mischief as my dad called it... when he used to talk about it."

We stop for the light next to Union Station. There are enough Publics and Shares here that it feels like proper traffic the likes of which I have not seen since leaving Seattle. The walk symbol lights up for us, but Hector remains still and says, "It's interesting, in a way, how someone who sought freedom can become so..."

He trails off and starts across the street as the walk symbol turns to the warning symbol. I walk with him. He goes quiet again, for about a block.

"Anyway. I go up to visit mostly out of guilt. And duty, I suppose. I read him his favorite poem, which I translated to Spanish for him. He knows English, just doesn't want to speak it since mom passed. He got fluent for her. I guess without her, he has no use for it."

What poem, I ask, as I am not sure what else to say.

"The poem I am soft of named after," he says.

I squint my eyes at him, trying to think of any poem I might know titled Hector.

He laughs. "My full name. Hector Ozan Walter Laureano."

That...is a name, I say.

He laughs. "That it is."

I think it through and ask, *Howl?*

"Yep. Like I said, hippies. I translated it to Spanish a few years ago as a way to try to connect since our falling out of sorts."

I am sorry to hear that, I offer.

"No big. Just...a difference of opinion about what kind of man I should be. I mean, I'm still trying to figure it out for myself, but I'm not at all convinced his way is right. I wonder sometimes if we were both the same age as I am right now...how we might communicate differently."

We start onto the bridge that goes across Naito.

"Shit. I feel like I'm talking too much," says Hector.

You are not, I assure him.

We stop for a few minutes at the middle of the *Steel Bridge*.

It is the best bridge in Portland. There are prettier bridges and bigger bridges, but this one does everything: Shares, Publics, trains, bicycles, pedestrians—those who walk and those who roll—and even we two, mildly idiotic fellows on the town for an evening out. And it raises and lowers for river traffic. It is the best bridge, full stop.

After staring at the water for a few minutes and mental soapboxing about a bridge, we continue across, then down the escalator that leads to the area underneath.

"Almost there," says Hector.

We walk past a small park, in a trapezoidal shape, that runs from the *Steel Bridge* to the building which I suspect we are headed. There are a lot of people in the park, or wandering at different speeds and modes along the riverside trail, enjoying the evening. We pass a sign, with a fresh pineapple resting on top of it, that proclaims: Welcome to Albina Town.

There is a mural on the building we are walking toward. From the roof to the ground, all eleven stories. At the top, in bold, purple letters with yellow-gold highlights the letters RTD. Beneath, a mural of a beautiful black woman in profile, her eyes closed, head tilted up and with a slight smile. It looks to me as though she is glad to be warmed by the sun shining overhead. Her afro is made of living plants.

"Welcome to the other side of the river," says Hector.

I realize that this is the first time I have left the west quadrants since arriving in Portland.

RTD, I ask, as we walk into the shade of the building on its north side.

"Right to Dream," says Hector. "This building went up a few years ago, replacing a camp for the unhoused. It's subsidized apartments that are mostly used by people who need a place to live while they rebuild. We're going to the club on the top floor."

It is a bit early to go clubbing, I say.

"It's a restaurant, too. And a music venue, a bar, a dance hall, and a community event space. So, club, not club," he says with appropriate emphasis.

I am not dancing. I only dance in specific instances, I say.

"You keep tellin' yourself that, man. Besides, we're gonna eat first, then come back later for the music. And dancing."

Bastard.

"What was that," asks Hector, the bastard who can obviously hear me, as he walks through the revolving doors of the main entrance.

I follow him inside. There is a circular information kiosk in the center of a large atrium with pamphlets, forms, and a smiling young man in the middle.

"Welcome to Right to Dream," he says with a slightly overemphasized dramatic sensibility. "I could tell this is your first time here by how long you was starin' at the mural," he says to me as my head tilts up and back to look at the five-story mural on the inside of the building. "Most folks pass it by who come here often. I wanted to make sure you got a good first impression. Hey, Hector."

"Hey, man. Howsit," replies Hector.

I wonder how Hector knows the young man, but not enough to ask about it. I wander the atrium to give them a chance to catch up. I look in the shops along the ground floor and note there are apartments which look into the atrium from the first floor and up.

The mural, above the shops on the river-side of the building, depicts, according to the placard I read, the story of the Right to Dream. From camps being torn down and built up again, to police raids—or "humane sweeps" according to a newspaper quote attributed to a former Mayor—and eventually toward the top-right of the mural with a group of people digging ceremoniously with shovels.

"Lotta history here, man," says Hector from behind me.

I turn to see him looking up, then back to me. There's something to his face, some emotion I cannot quite place without more context. Boredom, sadness, resignation. Pain perhaps. Hector sees me looking at him and replaces the emotions which I cannot pin down with a broad smile. And it looks genuine. I am not sure the extent to which I am terrible at reading faces or how good Hector is at channeling particular emotions when necessary.

"C'mon. Let's head up," says Hector.

At the top floor, the elevator doors open and I can see a mural running the length of the hall on the opposite wall. It welcomes us to *Roscoe's Skyline Cafe*. We step out and turn right, toward music. The double doors are open. There is no host waiting to guide us to a table.

"C'mon," says Hector.

He picks a table against the south wall. The view overlooks the river. We slide into the orange plastic benches. I look around the space and see a mix of up- and down-scale. There is a dance floor in the center of the room, though no one is dancing right now. Music plays over the sound system while people eat and chat. A few people are looking up at one of the two silent TVs which hang from the ceiling. They are laughing bawdily and watching *Cops* between mouthfuls of cornbread and ribs.

There are two menus on the table in front of us. The covers proclaim *Roscoe's Skyline Cafe* to be "the finest Soul Food restaurant on this side of the border." I pick up the menu closest to me and look inquisitively at Hector. He looks inquisitively at me as, apparently, my inquisitive look is not enough to convey what I am inquisitive about.

I point to the "on this side of the border" part of the menu's cover art.

"Oh. Borders are everywhere. You're always on this side of some border."

That explanation is adequate, I say.

"*Gracias*," says Hector. "Damn fine food though. And you won't need that, I'll order for us."

Hector takes the menu away from me as a server comes to the table. He sets down two glasses and pours beer from a pitcher into each. He leaves the pitcher on the table and stands perfectly still looking at the space on the table between me and Hector.

Hector says, "He'll have the Fried Catfish with Red Beans and Dirty Rice as the sides. Beef ribs and cornbread with greens for me. Oh, and we'd like barbecue sauce on the side of each plate. Thanks."

The server nods and leaves.

The music moves well into the background as our attention is drawn to those laughing at the antics on the TV. I glance around the room and note I'm one of the few white people here. The only others are a table of four dressed in military fatigues. I look out the window over the river, but each laugh draws me back in to the TV. Seems as if it is a regular thing to watch people try to avoid being arrested on a reality show while having soul food.

My stomach rumbles. I hear a "hey" from Hector and look to see our plates being laid out on the table before us. There is...so much food. Within a few bites, it is clear that this really is damn fine food. The fried catfish dipped in the barbecue sauce, extremely tangy and not at all sweet, is eyes-rolled-up-in-the-back-of-the-head good. Hector offers me some of his greens. They are bitter, not overly so, but not entirely to my taste.

I realize after a few mouthfuls that we have not talked since Hector ordered for us. I think about saying something, but decide another mouthful of the dirty rice is a better idea. Hector looks at my plate, then bobs his head slightly, asking silently if I like it. I point at the plate with my fork noting how half the food is gone already. The background music picks in volume up a little. *Cops* is over and the TVs are turned off. The view out the window is rosy-orange as the sun starts to set.

This is damn fine food.

Hector refills my beer and then his, emptying the pitcher. He puts it on the edge of the table and within moments it is taken away to be replaced by a new pitcher of beer. This place just runs.

As I shove the last bite of barbecue-sauce-dripping catfish into my mouth, a tall, wall of a man, wearing a spotless, glowing white apron, comes over to our table. He holds tongs in his left hand and a cooking pot in his right.

"You boys want some more greens?"

I shake my head no.

"I'm good," says Hector.

"Huh," says the man. "Y'all like the cooking?"

We both nod emphatically as our mouths are full of the final bites of our meal.

"Good. It's my place and I'd be off-put if you weren't enjoying it," says Roscoe.

We assure him that we are enjoying it.

"What are you boys getting up to tonight," he asks.

"We're here, then off for a wander, then back here when the floor's hoppin'," answers Hector.

I am trying to figure out what I should be doing with my life, I say, with a somewhat glib intonation.

Roscoe looks at me. He puts the pot of greens onto the table next to the pitcher of beer. The breadth of his shoulders seem to be doing their best to block all the light in the room behind him, though I can see his face clearly. His dark skin is heavily lined. Deep reddish-brown eyes around which the sclera shines as brightly as his apron. I can barely hear the music, as if his form is blocking that out, too.

"Listen, son. Everyone, at some point in their lives, needs to give themselves permission to flounder a while. I'm not talkin' about doin' nothin'. I mean flounder with intent. Forget time. Make no commitments that can't be broken. Make commitments and break them. Do everything that interests you. Do things especially in which you have no interest. Go well out of your way to do something you've never done before. I did all that, long time ago, and it felt good. I was lonely, a lot, but what of it. You hear me?"

I do, but how should I flounder with ... I let the sentence trail off.

Roscoe chuckles. "You need to accept some synchronicity into your life."

He picks up the pot and says, "Now. You boys want some greens?"

Hector and I both say *Yes, sir* at the same time.

This seems like the kind of place where if the owner comes out of the kitchen with the express intent of serving you up some food at your table, the only answer is yes. And yes, sir is more appropriate.

After eating all of my greens, regardless of the bitterness, Hector pays the bill. I thank him. We get up from the uncomfortable yet welcoming benches and walk back to the elevator.

Where to next, I ask.

"You'll see," replies Hector. He is clearly pleased with himself for keeping things a secret and not telling me what is going to happen tonight, beyond threatening dancing. Hector presses the down button and I look above the elevator doors.

Painted in a fluid, cursive script is a quote:

The most admirable thing about the fantastic is that the fantastic does not exist; everything is real.

The elevator doors open. We cross their threshold and descend.

Outside, the sun is still out but well to the west. It is warm still, though not overly hot and strangely quite humid. Hector walks toward the river without saying anything and I follow. We make our way back to the west side of the best bridge. It is somewhat busy with foot traffic and each Public that passes seems more full than is normal for this time of day.

We wander along *Waterfront Park* and eventually come to the *Burnside Bridge*. From behind us, I am almost run over by a bicyclist who is riding on the walking path instead of the path for bikes. In tandem, Hector and I each reflexively flip him off and Hector yells at him to share the road.

We continue south under the bridge and stop next to a very tall statue. It is 42 meters tall, according to one of the several bronze placards on this side of the plinth. We stay there for a bit, reading the large, encyclopedia-sized placards. The statue depicts Cenisa Goodwin whose actions as an activist and the first black, female mayor of Portland led to "structural policing changes" for the city. She adroitly and ruthlessly pushed the Police Bureau and the Police Association, publicly and on a daily basis, for the first two years of her term. Public shaming at that level and with that rigor, plus refunding of services that actually help people, allowed for inertia to change from stillness to motion.

Cenisa's statue stands with her right arm raised toward the sky, hand clenched into a fist. She wears flowing robes down to the knee, akin to the Statue of Liberty, and bare feet. Her left arm reaches back behind her, hand open. Given the height of the statue, her face and raised fist must greet people as they make their way into Downtown each day, reminding them that her hard work, use of the bully pulpit, and assassination allowed things to be put on the path toward change.

After circling the plinth, reading in silence, Hector pulls me along with a nod of his head to continue south. We pass a small group sitting at a picnic area and are singing. Joggers, less-selfish bicyclists, walkers, rollers... People are out to goof off in force—plenty of laughter. We continue, still in silence, for a few minutes, then Hector veers off the path toward the river. We walk on the grass, winding our way through the maze of those who relax on blankets, talking quietly or reading books.

Hector leads me to a folding table with a banner attached to it. There is a smiling young man behind the table. The banner reads: Raft Rentals. Hector puts two tens on the table while the young man attempts to engage him in polite, practiced conversation. Hector is having none of it and holds out his hand.

The practiced smile fades.

"Here you go. One hour," says the young man as he hands Hector a fob.

I shrug in mild apology to the young man and we all descend the stairs which extend off the park's edge, down to a dock where several rafts await. Hector presses a button on the fob and an array of bright pink lights, wrapped around the rectangle of the raft, flash a few times. The soft *hum* of the motor starts. Hector steps onto the raft and I follow. The young man unties a rope from around a small post and tosses it onto the raft. He heads back up the stairs without comment.

We sit and Hector presses up on the fob's toggle. The raft pushes away from the dock as the *hum* from the motor mixes in a high-pitched *whir*. The river is calm today and there is very little rocking as we watch the shore recede very, very slowly. Hector uses the fob to steer us south, paralleling the park. It takes us a good fifteen minutes to make it to the south end of the park where I can see a small beach area.

"I think I'm Penny Pretty, man. I need to be more Buckaroo," says Hector, interrupting his extended silence.

How do you mean, I ask.

"I'm down to my last nickel," he replies. After a beat he adds, "Figuratively."

He tacks, if one can tack without a sail, toward the middle of the river and brings my attention to a submarine docked along the shore, which is unexpected. Once we are in the middle of the river, he turns south again. We lean back in silence, floating forward under *Interstate Park*. We can hear children yelling from above. I look up and follow the trajectory of falling flowers which land in the water behind us. I can hear an adult yelling and can see the children who were peering over the edge of the bridge immediately scatter.

As we approach the north point of *Ross Island*, Hector says, "You can get away from home, or wherever, but you can't get away from yourself. And probably shouldn't try."

Hector's malaised tone make me tense some. A medical helicopter flies above. The sound of a gaggle of children yelling in delight comes from the west bank, near the tall apartments. From our vantage, Portland's west side reminds me a little of Hong Kong from *Victoria Harbor* and I wonder why I would think that. A boat speeds north along the river to our right. Hector steers the raft left and the island begins to reduce the impact of the speedboat's wake.

We've got to get you another nickel, so you can rub them together, I say with a smile.

Hector remains quiet. The air gets cooler as we pass along the edge of the island, the trees blocking the sun. He steers us around another point, then west again. We are technically in the middle of the river, but the view from here makes it seem like we are on a lake.

Without warning, the electric motor stops. The raft drifts forward a briefly, then lurches slightly as if we hit a sandbar. I look at Hector. He looks at me with a crooked smile, but his eyes hold a deep sadness. He pressed the toggle on the fob each direction it can go and nothing happens. We lay back and look up to where the stars will be in a few hours. A few minutes pass and the raft's pink lights return, blink twice, and are accompanied by a pleasant tonal melody. Which then melts into drowsy beeps before going silent. Thirty minutes have passed and the raft just told us it is time to head back—except Hector and I are not going anywhere.

We lay there in silence. Gray clouds start moving in slowly from the east, but at river-level there is not even a breeze. Even if we had a sail we would not be moving. The ambient heat starts to mix with a coolness that swirls around us. I stick my hand in the water to try to paddle us, but we remain stuck. Hector continues to lay back, looking up.

Sandbar, I say.

Hector does not reply.

I roll over to my stomach and inch my way toward the motor-end of the raft. When my upper arms are extended past the edge, I lean forward and submerge myself in an attempt to see what we are stuck on. Nothing. The water is clear here and I can see easily for at least ten meters.

There is no sandbar, I say as I reemerge from the water.

"Figures," replied Hector.

For the first time in my life, I am nonplussed—which I would be excited about—but this is confusing, I say.

"We don't have to do anything. We can just lay here and listen to the birds. To the kids on the shore. To the speedboats zipping up and down the river on either side of us," says Hector.

Sure, but eventually we have to go back, I say.

"Maybe," says Hector.

There is nothing I can think to do. Paddling doesn't work. There is no wind or current to push us in any direction. We are not actually stuck on anything. One-third of me is already wet so I decide to jump in and swim to shore. I stand and ready myself to dive off the raft.

"What are you doing," asks Hector, his voice rising and cracking. He sounds afraid.

I am going to swim to shore, cross that part of the island, then swim to shore again, I say.

"Fuck," he screams into the sky.

The pink lights flicker on once and turn off again. The water ripples, ever-so-slightly, away from the edges of the raft. I turn back from my diving pose to look at him. He looks ready to catch on fire. He is vibrating and his skin looks flushed.

"Fuck," he screams again, pulling the word the length of his breath. The pink lights come on and stay on longer. The raft moves forward slightly. The fob is still in Hector's hand, but he is not pressing the toggle.

You seemed relaxed up to now. What is wrong, I ask.

"Being still isn't the same as being relaxed," says Hector.

He rolls over to his stomach and pushes up until he is resting on his hands and knees. He begins to scream and intersperses it by yelling something in Spanish. Tears drip down his cheeks and onto the raft. The pink lights are back on and are very bright. The engine starts its idle *hum*. Hector hits the raft with his left fist and we jolt forward about a meter. Again he hits the raft and again we jolt forward. My knees buckle and I fall to the raft with absolutely no elegance.

I lay on my side facing Hector. He looks at me, his sclera red, a look of shame on his face. With visible effort, he coughs out a, "sorry, man" and looks back at the deck of the raft. The knuckles on his left hand are bleeding. Loud sobs are replaced with quieter choking sounds as he tries to find air. He falls to the deck of the raft with no attempt to brace for the drop. Ripples pulse away from the raft. I look up and can see the ripples his outburst created already bouncing back at us from the shore.

The lights remain bright and the *hum* from the engine is solid. I press the index and middle fingers of my right hand to the side of his throat. I can feel a pulse and can tell he is breathing, mostly steadily. His right hand still clutches the fob. I take it from him, return to a sitting position, and test the toggle to see if we move. Forward and to the left we go.

I look up as I notice a chill around me. The sun is still up, but the light is already fading. Dark clouds are moving in faster and faster. I steer us on a reverse course, back to the rental spot. I hug the west shoreline. The closer we get to the dock the more it feels like rain. We are able to go at the raft's full speed, but it still takes us close to twenty minutes to get back.

The young man is waiting on the dock as we pull in. He is wearing a raincoat and is decidedly not smiling anymore. The raft bumps into the dock and Hector pushes himself up to a kneeling position with a gasp, as if waking from a bad dream.

"I need to tie this up. Please disembark," says the young man.

I toss him the rope that is connected to the corner of the raft and we step onto the dock. I have to help Hector as he is wobbly in his steps. Hector pulls away from me.

"I got it," he says, shame still showing on his face and in his voice.

We walk up the steps to the rental table. There are very few people in the park now, only the ones with likely nowhere else to go. I guide us to a nearby bench. Drops of rain hit the ground here and there.

What happened, I ask.

Hector pulls a bandanna out of his pocket and wraps his left hand.

"I don't want to talk," he says.

He ties the bandanna off tightly and grimaces with pain. The rain picks up. I am still wet from the submersion and getting wetter. Neither of us are dressed for rain.

"I'll catch you. Gonna walk for a bit," says Hector.

He stands up and faces me. His eyes look less red but the remnants of tears are still obvious. He sniffs, nods once at me, and wanders south through the park. I feel abandoned and befuddled, but I let him go without delay. The rain picks up in intensity. I have a long walk ahead of me and will be beyond soaked by the time I get back to the apartment.

I jog across Naito then north. As I turn left on Flanders, I decide I am in no hurry. When I am back, I can take a hot shower and dry off. I slow to a walk along the north side of the street. Several people rush past me in both directions looking to get out of this surprise storm. The wind has picked up, too, and is blowing me along my route home. I get to 22nd and turn right, then left at Glisan. I walk past the thrift store which looks as if it has closed early due to the storm. I make it inside the apartment, close the door, and lean against it. I take off everything at the door. The blinds are open to the side entrance and I do not care. I walk to the bathroom and start the shower. I could get in right away, as I am cold enough at this point, but I wait for the hot water which I know will be two or three minutes away.

I look at myself in the mirror and reflect on the day, what little I understand of it. I wonder why Hector was so quiet and why he was so loud. I wonder why we were stuck dead in the water and why the engine decided to come back to life. I look at myself, shivering, yet stubbornly waiting for hot water, and wonder why I wonder these things.

I can feel a sense of familiarity creeping in. Walking the same streets, drinking the same coffee, having the same meals. It feels good and makes me itchy to move at the same time. I am continuously split. I keep hearing Meg's voice, though I suppose it is not as loud recently. That itchiness, which tonight pulls my attention more than the comfort of routine, leads me to think it is time again to make a move—and it likely does not matter the direction.

I put my arm into the shower and let the now-hot water pool in my cupped hand. I think about Hector walking away from me and wonder if he is yet out of the rain.

After a hot shower and dry clothing, I sit on the floor of my apartment. I look at the clock. The long walk home, along with the long shower, have it past eleven. Based on the time, sleep seems like the right thing to do, but I am feeling quite energized and ready to go. Somewhere.

The shower helped calm some of the intensity of the itch to move such that I do not feel compelled to leave Portland tonight, but within the week feels right. In the meantime, if sleeping is out, perhaps I should be out, too. I think about the welcoming feeling I had at *Roscoe's* and decide to return.

I check myself in the bathroom mirror to make sure I am publicly presentable. I ask my mirror self if we are really about to go out on the town by ourselves.

"By yourself," my mirror self says. "I am only a reflection."

I lock up and grab a Share as one glides by along Glisan—a gift to myself of efficiency, prompted by a recent bump in tip money. It is no longer raining and the lights of the city reflect off the low cloud cover to make the night seem as bright as when Hector and I first met up hours ago. The Share winds its way across the river and pulls into the drop-off circle at RTD. I put a few dollars in the payment slot and step out to see that there is more foot traffic than earlier—many people are heading into the building. A feeling of discomfort at being around people tries to catch hold. Again I am split. I want to be around people and I want to be alone. I consider sliding back into the Share, but surprise myself by walking in, letting the Share's door close itself behind me.

Up I go and I can hear the music coming from *Roscoe's* even before the elevator doors open. As they do, sound and light wash into the elevator. It feels almost tactile, as if there is a slight pressure stepping into the hallway. The quote above the elevator is now lit up with helium tubes shining out in a pink-orange light. I walk through the double doors, into *Roscoe's* proper, and feel like I am partially submerged in water again.

Besides Roscoe, who I can see, barely, at the other end of the room, I know no one here. The dance floor, the entire space really, is flooded with people. I stand still at the edge, essentially halfway in the room and halfway out, considering my options. I can feel the pull to leave; to go back to my studio, get into my sleeping bag, and go to sleep.

My right foot starts to take a step to the side in order to reverse course when my eyes are drawn to someone standing in the very center of the room. She looks up at the ceiling as if she can see through it, through the clouds, to the stars beyond. My foot stops moving, mid-step. A man appears in front of me. I squint through the auditory and visual sargassum and recognize him as the one who brought the beer and food to our table earlier.

"You lost, honey," he asks, though it sounds as if he is only slightly interested in the answer.

I shake my head no, but am not sure I mean it.

"Well, in or out and in's always more interesting," he says and moves past me, presumably to the restrooms down the hall behind me.

With him gone, I can see her again, though I begin to wonder how, given the number of people between us. She is still staring through the ceiling. She sways slightly, back and forth, not quite to the beat of the music playing.

As individuals, the people dancing around her move in jumps, spins, flings, and bobs, with hands and hair flying all directions. As a group, they rotate slowly around her, as if she is the source of gravity that keeps this world spinning. The music switches to a new song and the crowd howls in approval. Each person seems re-energized and the mass spins faster around its center point. Her slow sway remains unchanged and she is looking toward me now.

She raises her right arm, her hand palm-up, and she waits.

I take a step toward her. Then another. It feels like I am not in control of this reaction which alarms me and yet I also do not care. The spinning mass of the crowd weaves around me in such a way that I do not have to change my direction or pace and neither do the people dancing around me.

I raise my right hand to take hers and she smiles. My focus tilts to it as if I can see nothing else but her smooth skin and deep purple-adorned lips surrounding bright-white teeth. Her smile widens as I feel my hand take hers. She pulls me close and guides my right hand to her hip. We slow dance in a tight circle to a rhythm that is entirely out of sync to the one playing over the sound system which propels the crowd around us.

She shifts her head from resting on my shoulder to whisper in my ear. I cannot hear what she says, but can feel the pulse of her breath washing gently over my ear. I lean my head back, trying to watch her lips move in order to make out what she is saying, but she swings us around in a full circle. The crowd matches the movement, perfectly spiraling around us. One song flows into the next and she pulls away from me suddenly. We stop dancing, but the crowd around us continues faster than before. Mixed in with shouts of pleasure I hear a muffled pain. For some in the crowd surrounding us, this new pace is too much, yet there are even more people on the dance floor with us.

She twirls me then pulls me close up against her. She again whispers something I cannot make out, but three seconds later, like the delay on a long distance call, I hear her voice in my ear.

"I want to show you my favorite tree," says L.

I am not sure when she told me her name.

L takes my hand and leads me across the dance floor. The crowd separates ahead of us and closes in behind without a single misstep. We walk through the entryway and the elevator doors open as we walk up to them. The ground floor button is already lit. As we step outside, a Share pulls up in front of us. Two men get out and one holds the door for us to get in. We sit in the back together.

"Alberta Park," says L.

The Share pulls silently away from the curb to begin meandering its way to wherever this park is. We are quiet together, both looking out the window as the city passes by. At the intersection of Weidler and MLK, the Share begins to slow—someone is waving it down.

"No," says L, and the Share resumes its speed.

If there is an empty seat, Shares are supposed to stop, but according to L, apparently not. We turn onto 15th and even though it is my first time in this area, it looks somewhat familiar. We cross Prescott and Alberta, then turn right on Killingsworth. Very familiar.

"Getting close now," says L.

The Share turns on 19th and comes to a stop in front of a fire station. The curb-side door opens and we get out. Neither of us pay the Share, yet it drives away without complaint to wander the city in search of new passengers. There is a musk ox skull above the bay door of the fire station. It, too, looks familiar.

"Come with me," says L.

She takes my hand as she did on the dance floor and guides me along a narrow, paved path between the fire station and a tennis court. I feel as if I have walked through here before.

Big park, I say. Though mostly in order to prompt L to speak with me.

"Just the right size," says L.

We walk through some bushes and trees clumped together and into a relatively open field. There is a very, very tall tree in the middle and L guides us toward it.

"Have a seat," she says, as we arrive at our destination.

We sit. The grass is wet. A fog settles low around us, circling like the crowd at *Roscoe's*. There is light coming from a covered basketball court where a dozen or so people are playing. The light reaches us, but I can barely hear the people even though I should be able to as we are easily close enough.

L looks up at the tree and I follow her gaze.

"Do you know what kind of tree this is?"

I confess I do not.

"It is a Linden tree. Do you know what that means?"

I confess I do not.

The fog becomes more dense. The light cast from the court seems brighter, each lamp makes a halo due to the fog. The light is strong enough that I can feel some warmth from it. But the noises made by the players, still dribbling and shooting, are quieter still.

"The interesting thing about Linden trees is that they aren't classified as trees. They are poems. Do you know what that means?"

I confess I do not.

L leans back, pivots, and lifts her legs up to cross mine. She looks directly into my eyes and they are the color of crema on a freshly pulled shot of espresso. She smiles to herself as if an old memory surfaced suddenly.

"Elle se penche et m'embrasse, doucement, sous le tilleul," says L.

I tilt my head inquisitively to the right. L tilts her head to her right.

She leans in and kisses me, gently, beneath the Linden tree.

There is no fog. There is no light. There is no sound. There is no potential school or work. There is no past, nor is there a future. There is L and there is the Linden tree and I am between them.

L leans back, resting her hands on the grass behind her. She looks up again to marvel at the tree, as if it is her own creation. I follow her gaze and wonder how such a large tree can exist in a city. The root structure must be immense. I follow the trunk down and notice the bubbles and burls where it meets the ground. I imagine a mirrored shape of this immense tree, or poem, beneath the ground—*là bas*. I close my eyes and in my mind's eye follow the roots as they twist and branch through the soil and clay. I feel the vibrations of the worms and grubs moving along their familiar routes. I feel grounded and still. I could sit here on the grass, both above and below this tree, forever. This grass. The soaked grass beneath us. The soaked grass that is making my pants more wet by the minute.

The fog lifts and the shouts and laughter of the basketball players comes rushing in.

"Almost," says L, with a slightly disappointed sigh.

We should head back, I say.

"Dearest one...what one *should do* is so much less interesting than what one *is doing*."

MY eyes don't want to open.

When they do, I find myself shambling down 23rd to *Kornblatt's*. I need matzo ball soup. I don't recall drinking more than half of my second beer at *Roscoe's*, but I feel incredibly hung over. I need some food in me and I know my stomach can handle the soup.

It's busy at mid-morning. There's a line from the counter back to the ATM. This is one of the few places in the city that only takes cash and I do not have enough on me. I withdraw some money, note how little remains in my account, and wait to shuffle-step my way to the counter to order along with what feels like the rest of Portland.

Susan walks past me with a to-go order. She smiles and greets me with a nod of her head. We don't speak, which is fine as I don't feel yet like speaking. I need all the speaking energy I can muster once I make it to the counter. My mind feels foggy...drifty. I am not at all in a bad mood, but I also feel like I am missing something. I pat down my pockets and what little I carry, wallet and key, seems to be in place.

I get to the counter and order. I only have to repeat my order once—it's early for my voice and without caffeine, I tend to not enunciate. I am given a number placard and make my way to a table. I sit as still as possible as the air flows around me. The tables are only half full, but everyone is talking boisterously. Perhaps it only seems like it, but everyone is smiling. I look around the room again when I realize this. Everyone is smiling and laughing and listening to good stories being told. I sit alone, but it feels good to float along with the joy in the room.

The table has a fair number of postcards under Plexiglas. There is one in the middle of the collection of the Eiffel Tower with bright letters proclaiming PARIS across it—as if anyone could mistake it for another place. I think again of going there, then about the price of tickets in particular. Paris is on my mind and I feel the need to go there as soon as possible. If nothing else than to sit in a cafe somewhere, order matzo ball soup, and look down on a postcard that proclaims PORTLAND. Surely that Paris exists.

The server arrives and adorns my soup on the top of the Eiffel Tower. Best of both worlds?

So salty, I say after my first slurp of broth.

"Excuse me," asks the man sitting at the table next to me. His smile fades some and he sounds as though he's preparing to be offended.

Salty, I repeat, and point at my soup.

He nods, resumes smiling, and resumes telling his "why I learned to fly" story to his table mate. The window looking out onto 23rd is on the other side of him and my gaze lingers there as a young woman walks past the window, a grocery bag in hand. I see some coins drop from her hand and can hear them clatter on the pavement, even though the door is closed and the room is awash with stories being shared at the tables around me. She looks back but does not stop.

An old woman walking a few steps behind her takes the time to stop, bend down, and retrieve the coins that rolled closer to the building. A man in a long, red scarf and his lover walking behind the old woman watch what she is doing and begin picking up the change near the curb. The two parties look at each other then back at the sidewalk for more coins. From across the street, a houseless man leaves his cart and penguin-walks over in hopes of picking up some of the money. He's too late. Everyone goes their separate ways. Moments later, the old woman comes back to scan for more coins.

I take a few more spoonfuls of broth, then chance some matzo. So far everything is staying down and my headache's receding. I take another sip and suddenly think of L, then of Hector. The events of yesterday, if it was yesterday, come flooding back. Between slurps and bites I become convinced I'm missing something that is directly in front of me, but I can't see nor hear it.

I am distracted by a mildly alarmed and demanding, "Excuse me," and look toward the counter to see a man in a dark blue, full-length raincoat, the hood is up over his head. I look outside and note that it's a sunny day, as usual. He makes his way past the line to the front of it. He places a bill on the counter. The man behind the counter nods and takes a moment from serving waiting customers to put some food in a bag and hand it to the man in the raincoat. Neither of them talk to each other—there is only a nod from the man behind the counter as the man in the raincoat leaves.

I finish my soup, sufficiently warmed and fed—in the way that only basic food can do—and wander back to my apartment. As I reach into my pocket for the key, I can tell my pants are still wet. I twist at the hip and can see grass stains on my backside. Have I really not been home yet?

I go in and am reminded I never picked up the still-wet clothing off the floor from my wander through the storm. Definitely time to do some laundry. I change into sweats and a t-shirt, grab the rest of my laundry, and take it down to get the process going. I then come back and spend a few minutes tidying up what little there is.

I decide there is time before the wash is done to take a shower. As the hot water falls over me, I start to find more pieces, but still cannot recall anything between the kiss under the tree and matzo ball soup. I decide to stop trying to recall in hopes the memories come on their own.

I redress and flip the laundry to the dryer. I do not feel like waiting, so I leave the small banker's box I use for laundry under the dryer. No one else has stuff here, so I'll likely not get in the way and if I do, they can put stuff in the box. Assuming they know it's more laundry basket than recycling material.

I dress in being-in-public clothing and wander to The Place for caffeine. I set myself up at the table next to the window so that I can easily distract myself from writing by the passersby on the sidewalk. Before I can go to the counter to order, a man in a dark blue, full-length raincoat walks in. The hood is up over his head.

I look outside and note that it is still a sunny day and it is still well hotter than it should be at this time of year.

He walks up to the counter and Andragon moves over from reading the paper to start making a latte without asking for his order. She finishes and sets the to-go cup in front of him. He does not speak. He puts a dollar next to the register, takes his drink, and leaves. Without even a raised eyebrow, Andragon puts the dollar in the tip jar and goes back to reading the paper. I walk over to the counter and sit on the stool across the bar from her.

What, I ask.

She looks a little confused, so I indicate the direction of the door. She shrugs.

"Sleepwalking Man. He wanders the neighborhood from time to time. Comes in now and again, though I suppose it's been a while," she explains.

How does he get a latte for only a buck, I ask.

Again a shrug. "Far as I know, he pays a buck for everything he gets. He doesn't seem to take advantage of it, at least not here. Like I said, it's been a while since I seen him, but usually he comes in once a month or so. At least while I've been here."

How did you know what he wants, I ask.

"He's never said a word. First time I saw him in here, he came in and just stood there. I asked him a couple of times what he wanted and got no response. I poured him a cup to go. He set a dollar on the counter, took his drink, and left."

But now he gets a latte?

"I make him what I feel like making." She turns the page to the comics section and reads while she speaks. "I talked to one of the flower guys next door, and he said that he sold Sleepwalking Man a bouquet of roses for a buck. I guess he buys once a month."

Why doesn't anyone call him on it, I ask.

Another shrug, her answer for most everything. She sets down the paper, grabs a rag, and wipes up a small spot of coffee from the counter. I can tell she is thinking of what she wants to say to me. After a few moments of semi-absently wiping the counter. She stands up straight, though not unnaturally so, and looks at me—directly into my eyes and, for the first time ever, I'm gifted with her full attention.

"Look. Every single person you will ever meet existed prior to you meeting them. Their story started long ago and you have zero insight into it. I'm sure people have called him on it, but it's fine with me. I figure you can either choose to deal with him or choose not to. Michael says it's okay to serve him. Warren says no, but I never listen to him anyway."

I try not to listen to Warren, too. He's the other owner of The Place, but he's rarely here. He is an overly anxious fellow and it rubs off on everyone. I realize that is the most Andragon has spoken to me in one go. And then, in a very Andragon-like manner, she picks up the paper and re-engrosses herself in the comics. She is never one for subtlety when she decides she is done talking, which is the one thing about her I can appreciate. I decide to grab my things and go find Sleepwalking Man.

The sidewalks are crowded with people making their way to the neighborhood's many restaurants for lunch. The street swims with bicycles, scooters, and an occasional Share. As it's a hot, sunny day, I figure it'll be relatively easy to find a man wearing a dark-blue raincoat. I make my way to the corner of 21st and Glisan and turn north on 21st, looking into each boutique and eatery as I pass. I take a moment to purposefully stomp on a spray-painted stencil by some OCA sympathizer. I walk further and see no sign of Sleepwalking Man. Granted, I only walk up to Marshall, but there really isn't much past the hospital—at least nothing I have interest in seeing even if he is somewhere ahead.

I walk back down 21st on the east side of the street. I pass by *Cinema 21* and think about taking in a movie later. It's an art-flick place. *Tie Me Up! Tie Me Down!* is playing and who does not love a bit of Almodóvar? *Hombre Mirando al Sudeste* is also playing, but I've seen that already.

Back to Glisan. I stand in front of the *Blue Moon* and get hungry looking at the menu tacked to the door. Which means I must be feeling better, likely because I am on the move. *Blue Moon* is a good enough place for burgers and fries, but it's on the expensive side. *Mr Moto* is across the street—cheap, fast, and good enough for the likes of me. Bells jingle when I open the door and Japanese fast food aromas welcome me. Sleepwalking Man is getting a to-go bento box from the cashier. For a dollar.

He walks past me and out the door.

Since I feel I can actually eat, I get a chicken teriyaki to-go and then am back on the move in no time as *Mr Moto* is quick. It's still lunchtime, but most of the people have found a place to hide from their jobs and the heat for an hour. To my left, nothing. To my right, nothing. I think to myself: If I were a sleepwalker, where would I eat my bento?

I decide to head up to the *Rose Test Gardens*. It is quite a walk going up, but it feels like a worthwhile journey. I'll be able to eat my Japanese food amidst the noon-hour bus-load of tourists that will likely be up there. On Flanders I turn right and immediately notice Sleepwalking Man about a block ahead. I walk faster to catch up and pace him from about a half-block back. Up Flanders, down 23rd to that wonky intersection at Burnside and then another right. It looks as though he is heading toward the gardens, too.

We walk up the long hill in a distanced tandem. I stop a couple of times to rest—I find myself more easily winded than usual, still needing to recover some from recent events—but never let him get out of sight. At the top of the hill, Sleepwalking Man stops and sits on the stairs that mark the entrance to the gardens. He's breathing very heavily. I can hear his breathing, but cannot see his face as it is enveloped by the hood.

I walk past him and sit at the edge of the big fountain that's within speaking distance from him, but not so close that I'm sitting with him. While catching my breath, I think about how best to start a conversation.

Long climb, eh, I prompt.

Perhaps unsurprisingly, he doesn't respond.

We sit in silence. He eats from his bento box. I let my food sit next to me on the edge of the fountain as the very mild rigor of the walk up here has put me back to needing food with fewer ingredients. A few people wander by, going both up and down the hill. Tourists for the most part. Perhaps a few business-types on their lunch break. Two charter buses pull in nearby and out pour two groups of Japanese tourists, which then merge into one large group. A man with a small megaphone, if something mega can be that small, corrals the tourists, speaking Japanese. He has an orange flag rising up from his back. As one, the group moves into and around the gardens like a murmuration of starlings. There's some deep connection between Portland and Japan which I do not yet wholly understand.

I watch them wander together into the area of the garden above the amphitheater, then they break off into smaller groups walking in different directions—taking pictures and ogling roses, as is appropriate. After a bit, I realize I'm spacing out in the hot sun.

I look back at the steps. Sleepwalking Man is gone.

I stand at the far end of the counter, by the stage, staring at my cup. It sits on the counter in front of me, almost empty. White porcelain, stained ecru with a layer of residual crema ringing the lip.

"Michael said you know something about fixing cameras. I finished hanging my stuff and wanted to take some shots."

His voice startles me. The drone of the air conditioning in the room—thanks to the hot weather which continues to keep autumn temperatures at bay—plus everyone's voices, spoon clinks, and chair squeaks echo in the space in such a way that it is both loud and easy to tune out. That he got so close without me noticing makes me think I was far away, even though I cannot recall now where I was, but it felt warm and comforting, like being in a soft bed covered with a cozy blanket. But there was also a sense, fleeting now, of...hiding? Being afraid? Something about not being here.

Hi, I say, attempting to restart the can-talk-to-other-humans part of my brain.

I don't recognize him. He seems to clue in on my confusion and repeats what he said a moment ago. I look about the room and see new art. I didn't realize it was First Thursday yet again. It's nice to see that it's not photographs again, I say in my head, except also out loud.

"Again," he asks.

Nothing, sorry. I know a little about cameras. I can take a look, I say.

I look toward the front of The Place. The Necklace Man stands at the register glancing over at us, very obviously making sure we connect. I give him a nod and a pursed smile. I don't feel much like being social, but at the same time I don't mind helping.

What's your name, I ask as I take his camera.

I can change. Slowly.

"Jem."

What is wrong with it, I ask, holding up the camera for emphasis.

"Dunno. I was going to take some photos of the work I finished hanging, but it jammed after I took the first shot. It's a new roll, and I'm not even sure it took the picture," he explains with a shrug.

I move my cup out of the way and set the camera on the counter in front of me. I'm immediately overwhelmed with a sense of impostor syndrome. I do know about cameras, but not a lot. And his explanation leads me down the path that the problem can be anything.

I take the strap off and hand it back to Jem, then squat to get a different view of the camera as I start to poke at it. My hope is that my actions look diagnostic, but I am essentially stalling for time while the rest of my brain catches up and offers me a possible idea of where to start.

I'm about to spin the camera to look at the front when we are interrupted by Shane. Which means it must be near four in the afternoon, because Shane's shift starts at four—as does mine. He seems to know Jem pretty well. Shane does not say anything interesting, as usual, but his appearance does serve to remind me that it's a half-hour until I need to switch into work-mode.

As Jem and Shane chat, I turn dials and flip switches on the camera. I try to take a few shots. It clicks oddly and the film does not advance. Shane leaves and walks down the hall behind me to the small office in the back. At this point I begin to feel like someone looking over a car engine, trying to make it look like I can overhaul it, but really all I'm capable of doing is changing the oil.

Do you mind if I open it up, I ask.

His heavy eyebrows raise.

You'll only lose the first frame or two, I assure him.

"Uh, sure...okay. Go ahead."

I turn so he can see what I am up to. He steps closer to look over my shoulder as I pop open the back of the camera, revealing the exposed film and inner workings. I pull the film canister out and wind it back into its roll, save for a small piece so that it can be pulled out again, and rest it on the counter next to my cup. I make sure the lens cap is on, then set the camera on the counter, balancing it on its lens.

As I lean over the camera to take a closer look, Jem follows my lean and asks, "Are you and Shane going out?"

I stop mid-lean, stand up, and turn to look him in the eye. I look back toward the office, then back at Jem. Then I turn, lean back over the camera.

No, I say flatly.

"I'm sorry, I didn't mean to offend you," he adds quickly.

You didn't. Honestly, I say.

I try to be as earnest as I can, which works against me. Even though I do not take offense at the question, it sounds like I am trying hard to show how little offense I'm taking. He's quiet for a moment as I continue my investigation of his camera—twisting what can twist and turning what can turn. It's become even more busy in The Place. The Necklace Man is going full-steam at the espresso machine. Shane is starting early by clearing tables. With the all the extra voices and noise from the espresso machine, I cannot make out what Jem says.

What, I say, loud enough to let him to know that he needs to speak up.

He smiles and shrugs. "I was just saying that I didn't mean to offend you. Michael told me you were seeing someone who works here."

I stand up and turn to face him again. He backs up.

You did not offend me, really, I repeat.

This time I manage to sound like I feel.

I'm beginning to wonder though, if this will have to happen a certain number of times before it becomes a motif, I say, turning back to the camera.

"Before what becomes a motif?"

Everyone thinks I need to be set up with someone, I answer, as I lean again to poke at camera parts which likely have names.

Most of the tables in the place are full now, including half of the counter spots. What little in the way of clouds there are today move out of the way enough to allow the sun to reflect strongly off the windows of the building across the street, making the room seem entirely too bright. People walk by outside. Some dress in office wear, but most dress for the hot weather which is odd as, according to the paper on the counter, it is the first week of November.

The reflected sunlight helps me see something small stuck at the top of the sprocket wheel. I try to remove it—it feels like a piece of well-ensconced lint—but it will not dislodge. Jem sits down in the chair closest to the end of the counter, and watches me work. He talks a little about his show.

Above us, running the length of the counter, small plaster sculptures hang by fishing line. Each figure, seven in all, twists and flails haplessly in the slight breeze from the air conditioning. Their faces are etched with despair and remorse as orange and red flames lick at their falling, white-winged bodies.

Hanging on the red brick walls on the opposite side of the room are Jem's paintings. Oil on canvas. Abstracts. Blues, whites, yellows, and greens are the dominant colors. The paintings are full of texture and movement. From the size of the canvases, the amount of paint on them, and the low price he is asking, I doubt he is going to make back even half the money spent. It works against him to sell art this good in a cafe, but I expect this is his first show and the purpose is exposure.

Jem's profit will come from the sculptures. Wire, plaster, and a small amount of paint. There is likely a one-thousand-percent markup on them, and for the quality and detail of the work, seventy five dollars for the small ones, and one hundred and fifty for the big ones isn't too much to ask.

As I continue trying to pull the lint out, I tell him that I would buy some of his art were money not an issue.

"Money is always an issue," he says, resting his head on his fist.

I have mote of inspiration with how to remove the lint, though I also suspect I'm nearing my limit being gentle with Jem's camera and the drive to be done with it is winning. I dip the tip of my left pinkie into a bit of the crema on the rim of my cup. It will provide enough moisture—but not be actual liquid— to loosen up the sprocket. After some back and forth rolling of the sprocket, and adding more crema, it moves so that there is enough surface of the lint to grab with my nails and out it comes. I load the film back into the camera, confident in my ingenious fiddling.

I bet you hear that a lot about your work, I say.

He nods emphatically. "Yeah. If everyone, or even half of them, who said it actually bought something, I'd have no pieces left. And I'd have some money." The last he says with laughter.

I close the back of the camera and forward the film. I lift the camera to my eye and point it toward the front door. Then I take the lens cap off and suddenly it is much easier to see what I'm aiming at. As I look through the viewer I recognize a familiar, yet blurry form standing near the cash register. The form waves in our direction, then walks toward us. As I focus the lens, I smile and snap a picture to test the fix.

Jem turns to look where I am pointing the camera and nods his approval. "She's striking."

I nod as L sits down in the chair next to Jem.

Your camera seems to be working now, I say, handing it back to him.

He puts the camera strap back on and asks L if she minds if he takes her picture with the falling angels in the background. She says that she does not mind, but asks if he can do it later. The Necklace Man comes over and sets a cup of coffee in front of her. She reaches for it, but is looking at me.

Hi, I say with a smile.

She returns my smile. She mouths a few words as she takes a sip of her coffee, but I cannot quite make out what she says. Still standing near us, the Necklace Man begins to take off his apron. He catches my attention and asks, "You want this one?"

I begin to reach out my hand in answer, but Shane steps in between us and holds out a clean apron. "I brought one," he says proudly. I look between the two offered aprons and choose Shane's as he seems to care which one I choose and The Necklace Man does not. Shane leaves us to clear more tables of dirty dishes. The Necklace Man takes his apron and heads back to the office. Jem stands up and puts his arm through the camera strap, hanging it from his shoulder.

"Thanks for fixing my camera," he says. He smiles brightly. "If any of the angels don't sell, you can have one in return for fixing this."

In that case, give me another camera to fix and I will take the painting by the front window, I say with a smile.

I feel like I'm in a good mood. I feel suddenly connected to this place. The Place and the place it inhabits. It is a feeling that is in such stark contrast to before Jem approached me. What was I thinking about? It felt dissonant, but cannot even recall the general topic of my thoughts.

Jem walks over to the other side of the room to begin taking pictures of his work. It's the last time we ever speak, which is a shame as I like his art very much.

Shane walks up behind me. He carries dirty dishes on a tray with both hands. He bumps me with his hip and says, "Let's get started. It's First Thursday and if we don't start now the art crowds will never let us catch up." He piles the dishes in the bus tub and adds, while I put on the apron, "By the way, did you notice that cute guy sitting up on the stage?"

I turn to look and see the guy who I think Shane means. All I can do is produce a confused look for him as he as walks toward the register. I put on my apron and look back to L. She is resting her head on the heels of her hands, looking up at the angel sculpture above her. She sighs as if remembering something and feeling bad about it. I put on my apron and ask what her plans are for the evening.

"I'll do this and then I will wander and see what I see," says L.

As with most things L says, it makes the most sense when I do not think about it too much. I ask if she wants to meet up after I'm done working.

"Not tonight. We don't connect for a bit."

Shane calls to me from the register, giving me an order to make. I nod to him, then smile at L. She is looking up at the angel above her again, letting her coffee go cold.

I work more shifts than usual over the next several days due to people being out for one reason or another. When a day finally arrives that I have no obligations, I find myself back at *Powell's* standing in the M section of the Blue Room. I take a used copy of *Black Spring* off the shelf and place it with the copy of *Blue Highways* that appeared on the shelves since my last visit.

My plan is to purchase three books, so I continue my wandering up and down the aisles. There is plenty to choose from, it is *Powell's* after all, and after some weighing of options, reading of back covers and judging front ones, I settle on *Kokoro*. It is tempting to get another book with a color in the name, but *Kokoro* feels like a good fit.

Tips at The Place have been decent lately, so instead of heading to the registers, I wander over to the Poetry section at the outskirts of the Blue Room in case four books is better than three. On one of the shelves at eye-level, there are five books which are faced. A sign above reads: Staff Picks. The second book from the left catches my eye. The cover is blocked in red and there is a black and white picture of a Japanese man, woman, and child. The child is smiling and adorable. *Legends From Camp* by Lawson Fusao Inada.

I pick it up and open to the title page. It's an autographed copy and personalized as well. It must be a used copy, but nothing about it looks used.

For Denise—Thank you for all your efforts—for everyone!
~Lawson

There is a receipt from *Wessel and Lieberman Booksellers, Seattle* tucked neatly between pages fifty and fifty-one. I read the poem titled *Memory* which begins:

Memory is an old Mexican woman
sweeping her yard with a broom.

I close the book, leaving the receipt in its place, and add it to the small stack I hold with me. There's something familiar about this book which I cannot put my finger on. Not something in the past. Definitely something not yet. I suppose I'll have to wait and see. Four books seem like enough and thankfully each copy is used so I can afford to get all of them. I turn to leave the aisle to walk to the registers only to find my way blocked by Sleepwalking Man.

Well, not blocked entirely, but there's not enough room to get by without directly interacting with him. Being surrounded by books always makes me feel more quiet than I typically am, so talking to a stranger feels like too much of an ask for my brain.

I look behind me to find the way unobstructed. I begin to turn when I hear a grunt of "Ah" come from him. I watch him reach to a shelf that I would need a stool to get to. I'm able to see the title as he takes it down: *The Mabinogion*. He puts it under his arm, walks out of the aisle, and turns toward the direction of registers. I follow.

He continues through the Blue Room and finds his way through the maze of stanchions to stand in line to pay. Because I follow him from a distance, another customer enters the maze ahead of me. We stand there, waiting, and the person ahead of me turns with a look of disgust on her face. She pushes past me, ducks under one of the stanchion ropes, and looks through the greeting cards against the wall.

I move up, as one should, and immediately understand why she left. The odor emanating off of Sleepwalking Man is palpable to the point of overwhelming my senses of smell and taste. I clench my jaw and resist the urge to follow the woman with a sudden interest in greeting cards. We do not wait in line long as there are many cashiers. Sleepwalking Man is called forth to the cashier directly in front of him. She greets him with a smile as he shows her the book he chose.

"Perfect. I'll just scan that," she says as she reaches out to take the book.

He recoils. She looks confused.

"No need to scan it, Liz. It costs one dollar," says an older woman with steel gray hair and thick-rimmed glasses. She is standing behind Liz. She repeats herself as Liz looks confused. "One dollar. No scan. All good."

Liz turns back to Sleepwalking Man who is holding out his hand with a dollar bill neatly folded length-wise. She reaches out gingerly and plucks the bill from his hands with the tips of her index finger and thumb.

"Thanks. I hope you enjoy it," she says to him, almost as a question, as he turns and walks out the doors which exit at 10th and Burnside.

The woman who came up behind Liz pulls her aside and I am called to the other end of the row of registers. I pay for my books, thankful for coffee drinkers who tip well, and find my way out the same doors as Sleepwalking Man. As I pass Liz's station, I overhear her saying, "that's weird" to the older woman.

Agreed.

The intersection is packed with people. Burnside is a major road, relatively speaking, running east-west across Portland. As such, there are plenty of Publics and Shares, as well as a plethora of pedal-powered modes of transport rolling up and down it. Intersections like this, with plenty of local, iconic attractions, build up with pedestrians waiting to cross the street.

I can see the top of Sleepwalking Man's head, or more accurately the hood of his raincoat, on the south side of Burnside, walking west. I decide to parallel him on the north side of the street. When we get to 11th, he continues to walk west. Technically, I can walk the same direction to get back to my apartment, but I pause long enough to let him get well ahead of me. I consider how odd it would feel if someone followed me around town.

I look about, in case anyone actually is keeping tabs of my every move, and decide paranoia is not an attribute I feel like adding to my Rolodex of issues. I hold the four books I have with me close to my chest and turn north on 11th. I think about how hot it always seems to be here. I am in the shade of tall buildings, but even here it feels hot. I think about the smell of Sleepwalking Man and the smells of this part of the city as I hold my breath, as much as possible, walking behind the Weinhard's brewery.

I resolve to take a cool shower when I get back and feel thankful for the option.

RAIN, rain, rain.

Publics, Shares, and, unsurprisingly, very few bicycles splash along the wet, saturated streets. I walk against them down Glisan. The air is warm still, but the rain feels good and there's a comforting smell of petrichor. Thick, dark clouds cover the sun and offer a dim light by which to walk. After only a block, my hair is wet, my jacket is wet, and my shoes are soaked. I wonder if I should buy an umbrella, but given the predominant weather during my time here, why bother?

I'm on my way to The Place. The Necklace Man wants me to fill in for him for a few hours. I can use the money, I tell myself as a way to convince me to keep walking forward. I don't feel like being around people today for some reason I can't pin down—and I'm looking forward to it less with wet shoes.

But, before I can sub for him, preparations must be made. I'm going through a my-music withdrawal, so I reverse course and splash over to the music store on 23rd near Glisan to buy the only music fit for a day like this: *Just Coolin'* by Art Blakey and the Jazz Messengers.

I arrive at The Place a few minutes early. I shake rain off my jacket in the entryway, just outside the door, prior to entering. I chide myself for spending extra time in the rain and buying music instead of an umbrella. Within moments, I take over for The Necklace Man, who scoots out right quick, and I put in my music. The first few notes are heaven and my day turns from a droning-gray melancholy to a light-Blue Note funk—meh to umbrellas.

Most of the orders, what few there are, end up being to-go. I have the space to myself and decide to kick off my shoes and socks and wrap a clean hand towel around each foot in hopes my things will dry some. Surprisingly, my pants barely got wet.

Michael comes in after about an hour. I make him a mocha, my way, and we talk awhile about college, about me, and about me and college. It is both a boring conversation and necessary conversation for my brain to listen to. As with most things, I'm of two minds regarding more school—I get the point of organized education and I very much don't get it.

Michael leaves to run errands and I return to reading *Tropic of Cancer*—which always sits behind the counter, left by a customer well before my time here—while making drinks for intermittent customers. A latte here, a drip coffee there. It feels like the perfect day to sit here, listen to jazz, read, and watch rain fall. Only one person seems to want to stay with me. They sit at one of the window tables, reading a book which I can't make out the title of without invading their space.

I look up from my book as I hear the bells on the door ring. A man in his mid-thirties by the look of him, comes in, looks around, yells "Fuck them gays! Yes on 9!" He leaves with a resounding *whoop* and I can hear him shouting the slogan running toward *Durst's* as the door slowly closes itself. I look at the person sitting at the table by the window. She leans her head against the glass, seemingly trying to get a look at the yelling idiot. She looks over at me, we both shrug and go back to our own reading.

My eyes scan the words and after a moment I find I'm reading the same paragraph for the fourth time. I wonder why I'm letting the idiot disrupt my mood, but realize I'm not sure what my mood is or if I would notice if it changes. I'm not in a good mood or bad, though I'm very glad so few people are coming in today.

I feel quiet. My whole body is at rest. My arms, heart, legs, stomach, head, and every hair follicle. The title track of the album is playing and I find myself holding as best I can to this moment.

The bell on the door rings out again. I look up to see Myria scramble in and it disrupts everything. Long legs, tight jeans, tight white t-shirt, and black leather everything else. I feel my heart again and I become annoyed that she has disturbed my humors—which is entirely my issue and not hers—but I am still annoyed. She gets a drink to stay and joins the woman at the table by the window.

Another hour passes and The Necklace Man comes back. I head to the apartment to grab my writing stuff and a new-to-me book, *The Water Dancer* by Ta-Nehisi Coates—lent to me by a regular customer who thinks I'll like it. I find my pens and notebook hiding underneath my sleeping bag, which might explain why sleep is so challenging of late. I end up back at The Place—where else—to write and spend a quiet evening. *Just Coolin'* is still playing, which makes me smile. I try to write, then try to read, but end up staring out the window. The street lamps become the only light by which to see passersby.

The rain continues to fall, but seems to be slowing.

A woman comes in with Michael close behind. Over the next few minutes, while Michael is back in the office, she answers the phone and clears some dishes from a table near me. She seems to know Michael, but I've not seen her previously. Our eyes met as she walks behind the counter. I realize that I don't mean to be staring at her and look back at my book, feeling ashamed. More and more people come in over the next half-hour. The Place is filling up more than I'd expect, given the time of day and the weather, creating a stark contrast to my time here so far today and I decide to leave.

I walk the two blocks home, glad that it is no longer raining. Wet leaves on wet pavement *squelch* beneath each step. The thrift store stays open until eight on Thursdays, so it must be Thursday. It has two bicycles in the window which never seem to move, as well as clothing, furniture, and bad fluorescent lighting. Three older women, who are there almost everyday, chat behind the counter. I stop in front of the window to wonder about getting one of the bicycles. One of the women waves at me and smiles. I nod without commitment and continue the roughly forty more steps home.

Two people pass me before I reach the building's gate. A young woman carries her groceries in a small *Durst's* bag. She is bundled in a long, black, puffy coat. An old man, still going strong but weathered by the years, is not far behind her. He is stooped over, carrying a large, clear, plastic bag over his shoulder. There is not enough light to show me what was inside the bag, but from the way he looks in the half-light, the bag holds his life.

I look up through the thinning cloud cover, my hand on the gate to the apartment building, and can barely make out the moon. It's a full moon tonight. While others are driven to lunacy, I'm back to being unmoved and passive from the day's interruptions. I go through the gate, the outer door, the inner door, and put my key into the lock on my apartment's door. There is no resistance when I turn the key.

I locked the door. Positive. Yet, it is not locked. I open the door and walk in. My TV—a purchase I should not have made, but suspect I did out of loneliness—is gone. My pile of papers, books, and a short stack of music are not in their usual position. My sleeping bag is piled up and resting against the small refrigerator. Almost everything in the apartment, what little I have, is not in its proper place.

I spend a few moments looking around. The box the TV came in is gone, too, which makes me actually laugh out loud. Whoever broke in, took the time to put the TV back in its box—pieces of Styrofoam and all. They obviously rummaged through my small travel bag filled with odds and ends and took my pocket knife, but left the five dollar bill for some reason.

I call the police non-emergency number and explain the situation. They tell me someone will be over as soon as possible. Surprisingly, an officer is there in under five minutes. He asks me to find the building manager and bring them to my apartment. I walk downstairs to the basement and knock on the manager's door. I remind myself his name is Sherman thanks to the small sign to the right of door. When he answers my knock, I invite him upstairs to talk to the police with me. He does not seem surprised by this request.

Back in my apartment, the officer writes down the list of my stolen things. I make sure Sherman knows about it, too. I note that he does not offer condolences or make an attempt to write anything down.

"Gotta tell ya, you're likely not getting any of this back," says the officer as he leaves.

I think about the situation after the officer and Sherman leave. I lock the door every time I leave and every time I come back. The only time the door is unlocked is when I am going through it. This is no evidence of forced entry, so it has to be someone with a key. My brain reminds me that Sherman has a key.

It could be the previous tenant, as the locks are the same, but I blame Sherman. I check to make sure the lock is in fact locked several times before going to asleep. Given the size of this apartment, it is easy to roll over as I lay on my sleeping bag and look at the lock. No voice of Nina Blackwood and the sounds of music videos to lull me to sleep tonight. After looking at the lock the seventh or eighth time, I finally fall asleep. Within what feels like minutes, there is a knock at the door. I bolt awake, reach for the remote, remember there is no remote anymore, and sigh. The knock at the door repeats.

"Hey, man, it's Sherman."

I stare at the door and do not answer. I hear the side door open and see him peering through the window to see if I am home. I lay frozen on the floor.

Please go away, I say out loud, but very quietly.

After a few moments he leaves, down the steps and along the walkway that opens out to Glisan. I hear the heavy iron gate slam shut—not out of any anger, it is simply heavy enough that if you do not close it gently, it slams.

I decide to find Hector in the morning and tell him my troubles. I then think about how easily I could see Sherman through the window and realize it is morning. It do not feel as though a whole night of sleep passed, but it did.

After dressing in somewhat clean clothing, I follow the path out of the building that Sherman took and turn right down Glisan for the two-block walk to The Place. As I pass *Durst's*, I think about what I might need to buy for dinner tonight. As I pass the flower vendor, I think about flowers for L, whom I have not seen for weeks. As I walk into The Place, I scan the room for Hector or at least a set-up chess board.

Andragon is working the morning shift. I get a non-committal answer if Hector has been in. She remains ever unhelpful. If she had said, "Maybe I have, maybe I haven't. What's it to you," I would not be surprised.

I get a coffee to go and stand outside The Place, leaning against the wall between the window and door, trying to think where I might find Hector. The Necklace Man walks past me without comment. I watch him walk up the sidewalk and turn into *Durst's*. After a few moments, I decide to wander downtown hoping that synchronicity will be kind and I will meet Hector around the next corner I turn.

I spend the morning wandering with no pattern. Sometimes I stop abruptly in the middle of a block and reverse direction. Hector is not in front of me, nor behind me. I walk like this until around two in the afternoon and decide it will work better if I let it go and do not try to find him.

That will surely put him in my path.

IF the decorations around the city are any indication, the end of the year is in sight, which means I have some decisions to make. It feels like things are coming to a head. I do not work very often at The Place and do not put any effort into finding work elsewhere. I am very low on funds. School also calls to me, though mostly out of obligation. School requires money and, likely, will not be in Portland. I am having a should-I-stay-or-go moment this morning.

It is three days prior to the end of November. Three days prior to the end of a month is the day I must take money to Sherman and I am not overly enthused to walk down to his basement apartment. I still suspect he is the one who took things from my apartment, though I have no proof. I am also hesitant because I do not have enough money to pay rent.

On top of this, if I am going to move on from Portland, now seems as good a time as any. I have not interacted with Cairene in what feels like many months. The people I see at The Place are nice enough, mostly, but not enough of a draw on their own to keep me here. I feel abandoned by Hector and L, both of whom have seemingly disappeared. Now feels like the perfect time to leave and my emptier apartment means there are fewer physical tethers as well.

I spend an hour, plotting on paper, while drinking a not-too-terrible cup of instant coffee. Apparently, I cannot be bothered to walk two blocks east and get something far superior for free. I sit cross-legged on the floor and look over my notes. I am unsure where to go next if I do leave. San Francisco, Santa Fe, and Houston are all possibilities as I know people there and can stay for free for a few days at least.

I surprise myself by writing Alaska on the list as well, though this turns my stomach. It feels like it would be a step backwards. Regardless, I have a list of possible next destinations. I decide it is time to break the news to Sherman, that his favorite tenant to steal from needs to break a lease. I walk downstairs to the basement and knock on Sherman's door. It is open and he is inside laying on his bed. He looks over and waves me in.

I step into the room, also a studio, and look around. This is the first time I have seen inside. Usually he opens the door only enough to greet me and take my money. I make note of the type of TV he has and if there are any large, cardboard boxes lying around. There are not.

"How are you," he asks.

I am well enough, I say.

We stand awkward silence for a few seconds too long and both start speaking at the same time.

"So..."

So...

Sherman laughs. I try to laugh as well, but I am in too much of an introspective mood to be so obstreperous—or, at the very least, that is how far a jump it feels to be able to laugh at anything right now.

So, a couple of things, I say.

Sherman nods, waiting for me to continue.

I nod as well, though more to myself as encouragement.

Two things. One, I do not have enough money to pay for the entire month of December. Two, I am not sure I will be here for the entirety of December, I say.

Sherman smiles. "Well... what can you pay," he asks.

I can swing about one-quarter of the rent, I answer.

"I see," he says. "Got anything else besides money," he asks.

I squint my eyes, in my usual fashion, which is a mix of trying to understand something and focusing my vision so that I may see better. It does not help, but it is a long-running habit. One which tends to make most people think I am angry. A thought of saying, Well, you already have my TV, comes to mind.

Sherman tilts his head to one side as if trying to figure out what my face is saying, but he waits patiently for my answer.

How about a poem, I offer.

"A poem," replies Sherman. "What kind of poem?"

Back to squinting.

A poem-poem, I say. No specific kind. I will write something for you.

"Uh, that's not how the world works," he says.

Why not, I ask.

Sherman pauses as if stumped by my question. I did not deliver it sarcastically, but instead with actual curiosity. He starts to speak, then stops, then starts again.

"Well, how about instead, the world tends to not work like that. Is this because of the break-in?"

I start to nod then turn it into a side-to-side motion.

Well, not really. The break-in was annoying—I know I locked it. Mostly it is because work is scarce and I need to head home. Family stuff, I explain, lying to him.

Well, a partial lie. Work is scarce—when you do not look for it.

Sherman nods and steps over to his kitchenette to grab a glass of water. He pours it slowly from an open pitcher that sits on the counter. He takes a long drink. I feel the urge to ask if he wants milk instead as he seems to be milking this moment.

He puts down the glass and wags his right index finger at me.

"Tell you what... you got a deal, but I have to like the poem."

I shake my head.

No. A poem can be great and you still may not like it. Eighty-two fifty and a poem, I say.

He smirks. "Okay, kid."

I hand him the eighty-two fifty—roughly half the last of my money—and wander back up to my apartment, grab my usual out-and-about things, and walk to The Place to ask Michael for a few more shifts to at least cover being able to eat for the next couple of weeks. Shane tells me that Michael is out of town until tomorrow. I make a plan in my head to come back first thing, then sit to write Sherman's poem. I do it in the time it takes me to drink a latte and have it still be hot when I am done.

I walk back to my building and make my way down to Sherman's apartment. I knock on the door and it immediately swings open. He must have been standing next to it. He looks surprised to see me holding out a piece of paper. He takes it from me, letting the door fall closed, but catches it with his foot. I can only see his foot and part of the piece of paper. I hear him chuckle softly, then say, "A what," then a quiet, "Huh." The paper falls from view and the door opens back up.

"When did you write this," he asks.

A few minutes ago, I answer.

"Huh. Well, this'll do."

He moves his foot and lets the door close with a soft clack. The poem got me out of paying full rent, but I feel a little let down in his reaction. I do not need him to like it, but getting a "Huh" makes me wonder what he thinks of it. I suppose, sometimes, there are things in like you are left with not getting to know.

Was This a Moment?

This is a moment
as is this and this and this

Sitting on this beach
I watch the waves work away
I feel the rocks and sand beneath
me and
they are comforting

Resting on these rocks which keep
me held to this spot as
I am nowhere else

Walking from the surf is an Asaro Mudman
he points the tip of
his spear in
my face and says in a language which
I cannot understand

Searching far and wide for
my long-lost soul has brought
me here. Might
you be
he

Crying
he takes offense as
I reply
I am not
I have been lost only a short while

"ONCE you find your quadrant, you never leave," seems to be an unofficial Portland motto. And why would you? The intentional design of this city, ever-aspirational and always half-finished though it is, puts the focus on the hyper-local—everything one typically needs within a mile of home. Or, within a mile of where you sleep, which I note here specifically because L and I are currently waking along Waterfront Park—the home of many people. I half-expect to see Sleepwalking Man.

I met L—seemingly by chance, though I sense she was looking for me—as I wandered the northwest grid in search of Hector. I am losing track of time again, but I know it has been weeks since I have seen him. There is never an answer to my knocks on his apartment door and he does not come to The Place anymore. I chanced to see the woman who lives and works in the adjacent apartment. All she offers is a shrug and a "soh-ry"—condolences with a Russian accent.

L was standing in the middle of the small park between Glisan and Hoyt near The Place. She was looking up at the sunny sky in much the same manner as the first time I saw her at *Roscoe's*. She held out her hand to me, still looking up, and as I took it, towed me along toward the river.

L suggests we sit on a bench in order to "watch the water flow by me"—I find her turns of phrase to be quite odd—and do some people watching as well. We find one nearby that is available and not plastered with bird excrement. Half the view is taken up by the statue of Cenisa, which means we are technically in Southwest and I am technically outside of my quadrant.

L sees me staring up at the statue. She follows my gaze up.

"It's an overly contrite apology, but I'll take it and all that comes from it," she says, answering a question I did not realize I had.

A few minutes of silence go by and L comments on a jogger going by, "I wonder who she is running away from."

Or running toward, I offer.

"No. No human runs toward things. Humans only ever run away."

L returns to contemplating whatever is truly on her mind. I think to myself, surely not all people run away. L seems ready with an answer to my unspoken question.

"I want you all to stay forever, but I've learned that many of you need to run away before coming back to me."

After some amount of time, we find ourselves walking up Ankeny, only a few blocks from the river. On our right, a garish display takes up the entire front window of a shop. A sign above the window reads: *The Church of Elvis.*

What is this, I wonder aloud.

"It's a church of course. And the best kind, too," says L.

Best kind, I ask.

"There is no pretense here. No one hides the fact that what will save you will cost money. And they don't dare tell you what will save you. They start by being honest and asking, '*Que voulez-vous?*'"

There is a sign on the building's facade which invites passersby to offer a tithe of one quarter receive the teachings of Elvis.

"Do you have a quarter," asks L.

Her tone makes me suspect she already knows the answer.

I have exactly one quarter. My last one. How lucky, I say.

I dig around in the left, front pocket of my jeans and pull out the quarter. It is dull and has been in circulation for so long I cannot make out the minting date, but it will suffice for a fortune.

L seems to mimic my rummaging and, instead of a quarter, pulls out a hair clip which is long and white with a sparkly, green fir tree on it. She puts it into her hair with no attempt to hold it back or down, but simply to adorn herself.

She looks at me expectantly. I turn to the wall, insert the quarter, and twist the knob. On the fifth go-round, I hear a soft *klack* and open the little door to reveal a plastic egg—yellow at the top, red at the bottom.

"Open it. You'll like this one," says L with a slight nod. Inside, a smartly-folded piece of paper reveals:

Neuer Frühling gibt zurück, Was der Winter dir genommen.

"See what I mean," she asks.

I do not, I say.

"You'll see. Be patient."

I look down to reread the fortune, forgetting, again, that I do not understand German.

Shoes so bright, blue, and suede come into view. I look up and Elvis is standing directly in front of us.

"Mornin', y'all. What do you want? Lookin' to get hitched?"

L looks at me. "See what I mean," she asks again.

She nods at Elvis. I find myself nodding as well.

Elvis nods, too, and says, "Let's get shakin', then."

We move out of the way of others waiting to receive the blessings of a coin-operated vending machine. L stands to my right and puts her arm in mine. She smiles at me. The whiteness of her teeth beam more for the smooth, dark skin that surrounds them. She wears only eyeliner, and only on the bottom lids. The fir tree in her hair sparkles radiantly. I find my eyes darting between her smile and the hair clip.

Elvis begins what feels like a well-practiced recitation.

"Alright, you two. Since love brought us all together on this beautiful, sunny day, let love guide us forward from here, uh-huh-huh. What's your name, son?"

I tell him.

"And yours, darlin'?"

L looks at him and smiles.

"Thank ya, lady," responds Elvis, as if a smile is enough of an answer. "The Church of Me blesses this union between the two of you. No distance between shall estrange the love here shared. Be it so, uh-huh-huh."

Elvis puts his right hand on my left shoulder and his left hand on L's right shoulder. He looks us both in the eyes and says, quite solemnly, "Now, git."

He turns and goes back into the shop.

L lifts her hand to turn my face toward hers. She pulls me close and kisses me gently on the lips.

"For what comes next," she says softly.

She releases me, turns, and walks west along Ankeny, turning out of sight as she takes a right toward Burnside.

"Hey, could you move a bit, buddy?"

A man catches my attention and I realize I am in the way of him and his wife getting their picture taken with Elvis with the entire shop as the backdrop.

Of course, I say, and move out of the way.

I feel drawn to follow L, but I do not.

Each time we have met, it feels like it is because she is seeking me out. Each time we part, it feels like she is done with me. I walk up Ankeny as well, but turn left toward Pine. I realize I am smiling. I am married. I stop walking. Am I? I doubt *The Church of Elvis* holds much sway legally, but perhaps that does not matter. L loves me. Does she? And what is coming next?

I turn to look back up the street hoping to see L, but it is only the regular mix of people wandering about during the lunch hour. My smile fades. I suspect I will never see L again, if I ever saw her in the first place. I am the one planning to leave, but it feels like everyone else is disappearing.

I realize I am still holding the plastic egg with the German fortune inside. I look at it again, chide myself for not speaking all languages, fold it neatly, and place it in my right, front trouser pocket. I snap the egg back together and lay it in one of the bubblers to float around and be a surprise for the next person to wander by seeking a drink of cool water.

I wake with a sore throat.

I hate being sick. It is a waste of time. I rarely get sick, but when I do, it tends to be bad. Cough, cough...wheeze, wheeze. I wanted to go to the PSU library today. Not anymore. Instead, I will lay on the floor of my apartment. Perhaps I will chance The Place for caffeine. I figure if I can summon enough energy to get up for the bathroom, I might have enough to walk a couple of blocks.

Tomorrow, I note, as I lay here whinging to myself, is Xmas. For me, there will be no mashed potatoes, no turkey, no peas to mix with my potatoes that are covered in gravy—which is the best way to eat them. No presents. No tree. No snow. On the other hand, there will be no snow.

I crawl to the tiny refrigerator and find it is a toss up between a potato I can bake and leftover vegetable soup. The potato might be ever-so-slightly more festive—if a potato can be festive. I hear that there is no proper way to celebrate something which makes you happy, so perhaps a potato can be festive.

I set the potato on the counter so that it comes to room temperature prior baking it later tonight—assuming I will be able to eat it. Ideally, something during the several hours between now and then will cure me. There are two small discs of butter, each wrapped in coppery-gold foil, in the fridge. I suspect I they come from *Kornblatt's*. I place each on the potato to also warm up. A russet orb adorned with bricks of gold will have to suffice for festiveness.

I spend the next few hours laying on the floor, shivering and sweating in unpredictable order and duration. At some point I sleep and eventually wake with a headache to top everything off. I suspect the headache is due to a lack of caffeine. I try pulling myself together enough to wash my face in the bathroom.

I crawl first, then pick myself up with the door frame. I run the sink to start the process of getting hot water—which for some reason always takes five times longer than getting the shower hot. I look in the mirror and tell myself I am not addicted to caffeine. Mirror Me does not agree and urges me to address this issue presently.

I wash my face, get dressed, and shuffle down to The Place. I have to stop a few times to rest and recover from shuffling slowly.

"You look great," says Andragon with obvious sarcasm as she turns to make an americano for me.

Michael is there, sitting at the far end of the counter. He waves me over and invites me, if I am feeling up to it, to do the Xmas thing with him and his family. I feel immediately on the back foot. I offer him as nice a thank you, but no thank you as possible, noting that I am not well and will likely not be much better tomorrow. I clamber up onto the stool one over from him and hear the bell of the front door ring out. The Necklace Man walks in and beelines with obvious intensity to where Michael and I are sitting.

"Did you hear," he asks. His brows are furrowed and his cheeks are very pink. He pulls out the stool next to me to stand closer to the counter, but does not sit down.

"Hear what," asks Andragon with a tone of well-practiced disinterest baked into the question as she sets my americano in front of me.

"Hector's dead. He killed himself. They found his body in the river."

We are all silent together for a few moments. No one makes eye contact. Andragon breaks the silence with a "Well, fuck..." that is filled with some of the first non-derisive emotion I have heard from her. Tears well in her eyes and she leaves us to go to the restroom.

A regular customer comes in and stands at the register, looking toward us with obvious interest as to why one of us has not come to their immediate aid. Michael pulls himself together enough to go help them, leaving me and The Necklace Man on our own.

"Fucking terrible," he says.

Yes, I say, and hold my cup to my lips. I take a tentative sip. It is bitter. And hot. And is exactly what I want in this moment.

Bitter, I say aloud.

The Necklace Man nods and leans back into the stool behind him. We sit in silence for a while. Michael comes back to us after helping the customer.

"I'm sorry," he says.

I stare into my drink watching the crema slowly rotate due to the heat of the liquid. I am unsure if he is saying it to me, to us, or in general.

"Yeah," says The Necklace Man.

I nod. I hold the hot cup in my right hand, against my chest. The cup is hot enough that it hurts my chest and my hand feels like it is burning. It hurts.

Michael and The Necklace Man begin to share their thoughts about Hector. I do not listen with much attention, but put together that The Necklace Man was looking for Hector for some reason and ran into one of Hector's brothers clearing out his apartment. I did not realize he had family besides his father, which is to say, I never asked. I continue to hold my cup to my chest until eventually it loses its heat and I can no longer feel anything. I set it on the counter and excuse myself.

As I arrive back at my apartment. I stop to check the mail because it seems to be one of those rare days when I get mail. It is difficult to open the small door. One piece is a college catalogue, and the other is a college application form for a different school. Both barely fit into the mailbox. It seems as if the mail guy looked at delivering today as a "challenge accepted" moment. I spend an actual five minutes getting the mail dislodged. Most of that time is spent leaning against the wall, barely keeping myself upright. Retrieving the two pieces of mail saps me of the last of my energy.

I unlock the door—definitely locked—and toss the mail on the floor where I might put a table, if I ever get around to finding one, not that one is needed at this point.

I crumple to the floor in the middle of the room, mostly on my sleeping bag. I crane my neck, too tired to roll over completely, and look at the potato sitting on the counter with the two gold bricks of butter resting atop it.

I imagine Hector laughing at me while I leaned listlessly against the mailbox, attempting to regain my composure from my asynchronous duel with the mail guy. I could use Hector's laugh right now.

I will never hear it again.

IT is, officially, the worst Xmas.

Alone and sick, my entire body is in constant, low-level pain. My main exercise is moving back and forth to the bathroom from my spot on the floor in the middle of the apartment. It is the worst Xmas because I have no one to take care of me. No one to tell me I am going to get better. To say they are there for me. To do nice things like get me juice or fluff my pillows. Rub my chest and stomach.

At some point in the late afternoon, I decide a food attempt is necessary. I put the potato and butter back in the fridge and try some vegetable soup— it stays down. After a while, I feel like I have more energy and less need to stay close to a toilet. I am craving comfort and decide that can be best had by pie, which I remember is in the freezer. I preheat the oven, put the small pie in, and lie back down on the floor.

Halfway through the baking process, I open the oven door to spin the tray so that the pie can cook evenly. I grab the edge of the pan to spin it— without an oven mitt. In one second, the tip of my right index finger is red and white, burnt flesh. I run cold water from the tap, leaning on the counter and stomping on the floor in pain and frustration with myself. The shock of the burn triggers the low-level pain I have been feeling to flood back in and spins my stomach in circles.

I put ice cubes in a plastic bag and return to laying on the floor with my hand on my chest and the bag of ice on my hand. After a few moments, I realize the bag has a hole in it. Water drips all over me, the sleeping bag, and the floor. For the next three hours, I stick my finger in the ice tray, which sits on a not-hot baking sheet, moving my finger from cell to cell, trying to find enough cold to combat the heat.

Fuck it, I yell to the room, after three more hours of attempting to doze.

I say it many times, trying different intonations and inflections, but the pain and frustration do not subside. It is well into the evening and I lay there in the dark, on top of my damp sleeping bag. My face is buried in the crook of my left arm and I try to convince my mind that there is no pain. I count to a hundred. I breathe. I repeat, over and over, there is no such thing as pain.

And then I decide to let the pain be painful.

I stop chastising myself for being so stupid as to grab a hot tray. I refill the ice tray and put it in the freezer. I run warm water instead of cold over my finger, then wrap it in a wet paper towel. I lay back down and rest my right hand on my chest. Not long after, I fall asleep. My final thought before drifting off: perhaps, even though I am leaving soon, I should buy some oven mitts. Probably as useful as an umbrella.

A week passes and I am finally well. My finger is still in a bandage, which I decided was better than a wet paper towel, and mostly it does not draw my attention much—only when I change the bandage each night. Since Xmas, I have barely left my apartment. I left twice to get new bandages and a little food from *Durst's* and only once to go to The Place.

I did not feel like being there, but eventually the lack-of-caffeine headaches were too much. I went in and there was someone new working. That made me feel worse in a way. They hired someone new and it was not me, likely because I am not actually here.

Today, I feel well enough to escape to *Escape From* for a slice of pizza. Crazy Woman is there and asks how I have been. I do my best to be polite, as she is doing nothing wrong by asking, but can muster little information for her as I have not been up to much and have no idea what comes next.

I need to find a new place to live, I say.

"Where do you want to move to," she asks.

I stand there, holding my hot piece of pizza—with my non-bandaged hand—and think about it. None of my options sound appealing and I will not have an apartment in three days.

Inconclusive, I say.

"You'll figure it out," she says and shoos me along so she can help another customer.

I eat my slice on the way back to my apartment instead of staying. Once in the main door, my attention is drawn to the mailboxes. I can see into all the slits of each mail box. Other people have white, yellow, and red bits of paper in theirs. I look through the slit in my mailbox. No colors. Only darkness. But today, I open the mailbox anyway, out of sheer hope that there will be a special message just for me.

There is a small, plain envelope with no stamp and my name written on the front. It is sealed. The envelope is wedged into the mailbox door on the inside. Of course I would not see it looking through the slit. But I never open the door unless I can see something other than darkness, so who knows how long it has been there.

I take the envelope out and have to apply a little force to do it, as if it does not want to be read. I look at my name written on the front. I do not recognize the handwriting. I decide not to open it. At least, not while standing in the hallway. Something about a hand-delivered note feels strange and intimate. My name is on it, but it does not feel like real mail if it does not come with an address, a stamp, and the extra ink added by the mail processing machines. This is a note. Notes should be hand-delivered.

I tell myself I cannot open it right now regardless as the bandage on my finger will make it difficult. I resolve instead to distract myself with other things for a while. I lock up the apartment and check three times it is locked—not that there is much left for Sherman to take. I decide to walk up to the *Rose Test Garden*. It is a sunny day, yet again, but not overly hot. The city feels very quiet, even though it is almost noon.

I walk along 23rd toward Burnside and find no obstacles. No one coming out of shops, no one going in. No one walking their dog. I take the jog up Westover to 23rd Place and stop in front of *Twist*. No one is inside, even though the doors are wide open. I continue across Burnside without the need to wait for bicyclists and the like. A solitary, empty Share passes me, going toward downtown. It moves very slowly as if hoping someone will flag it down and go on an adventure.

I walk along the forest trails where I can, and along the neighborhood streets where I need to connect between trails. No one is out doing yard work or jogging. No movement at all, even from the wind. I make my way to the far side of the oddly-empty-of-tourists gardens to the somewhat secluded area of the *Shakespeare Garden*. I pass a sign that tells visitors the plants here are all ones mentioned in his works. The plants are well-kept and organized and everything is just so, as the saying goes.

I find a bench easily enough as I have all of them to choose from. There is no one in this part of the garden either.

I am alone.

I open the envelope with my left hand. There is a single piece of paper, folded once along its width. I unfold it to reveal a short message, written with a marker, blocky, and in all-caps:

I'M WITH YOU IN PORTLAND. —H.

I spend my last morning in Portland packing up my things and cleaning the apartment. I pack my backpack as per usual—heavy things on the bottom, lighter on top. I walk down to the rubbish room to find a couple of cardboard boxes. Sherman's apartment looks directly at the room, from the other end of the hall. His door is open and his TV is on. I can hear Martha Quinn promising viewers that at some point she will learn all the lyrics to *It's the End of the World As We Know It*. It's probably something I should add to my to-do list as well. One never knows when it will be handy.

There are plenty of boxes to choose from in the rubbish room. I grab two banker's boxes and head back up to the main floor. I pass the mailboxes along the way, glancing at mine only briefly. I am leaving. There is no need to look inside.

I set the things I will take with me by the door and begin to divvy the rest of the stuff between the two boxes. I still have the poster tube for the *Fugazi* and *Moloko and Ultraviolence* posters I have up. I roll both of them up together and slide them into the tube. I am not sure why I decided to have posters up, beyond interrupting the plain, white walls. I am not a big fan of *Fugazi* and milk unsettles my stomach more often than not these days. I suppose it was art I could afford.

I put the kitchen utensils and other sundry items in the boxes, as well as some of the still-usable bathroom items. I unplug the phone from the wall and put it into the box, too.

"It's handy I wandered over instead of calling," says a voice from my doorway.

I turn with my heart racing. I did not hear anyone in the hall and did not realize the door was open. Susan is standing there.

"I hear you are off," she says.

Usually am, I say as my heart begins its decent.

This elicits a chuckle from Susan. "You know what I mean."

Yeah. Leaving tomorrow, I say.

"Are you taking everything with you," she asks.

No. These boxes are staying. I may—I put heavy emphasis on the word—come back through in the near future, so I was thinking about taking this stuff down to The Place and storing it in the attic, I explain.

"The place," asks Susan.

I realize I only call it The Place to myself.

Renaissance, I say.

"Ah."

She walks over to the boxes and begins looking through them.

"Can I take this spatula," she asks.

Sure.

"Oh, and this spatula, too."

Fine. Anything else?

"No. That's good."

She takes both spatulas and ties them together with a hair tie, then shoves them into the long, hip pocket of her overalls. Then she takes the oven mitts which I bought too late to do anything with.

"I didn't stop by solely to steal your utensils. I figured I'd check on you to see if you wanted to talk."

About what, I ask.

The question causes Susan's left eyebrow to reach for the ceiling—which clues me in on what she means.

Oh, no. Not really, I say.

"Okay. I've got a little time before band practice if you want help packing."

I look around the room. There is a plastic bag that needs to go down to the rubbish room, but beyond that I am done packing.

You have arrived just in time to not have anything to do. But thanks for the offer, I say with fake earnest enthusiasm.

"You are most welcome," she says with a bow and a flourish of her hand. "It is my superpower. Show up just when I am no longer needed, but make it clear I am there to help."

I roll my eyes at her which makes her laugh.

Well, you can take that to the rubbish room in the basement, or help me take these boxes to The Pl... to Renaissance, I say.

"Easy-to-lift boxes or creepy basement," she says and trails off. "Tough choice."

Fair, I say, picking up the bag of garbage.

I take the bag downstairs—this time it is quiet, though Sherman's door is still open—and toss the bag into the bin. I pause in the hall and think about giving Sherman my key right now, but more than likely I will need to stay one more night here and leave town in the morning.

Back upstairs I find Susan leaning against the wall by the doorway to the supposed walk-in closet and bathroom. She is holding one of the boxes. The lightest one based on how easily she holds it. I grab the other one—immediately sure she has the lighter box—and make a *this way* motion with my head. She waits in the hall while I lock the door and we walk out of the building and turn right on Glisan.

As we pass the thrift store, Susan asks, "Sure you don't want to drop this stuff off here?"

Nah. Like I said, I might be back and I'll want to have it, I say.

"Cool. So, I suppose that means I can't take the baking sheet, too?"

I immediately burst into laughter. I have to stop walking for a moment and put the box down.

You are more than welcome to take this cursed sheet, I say.

It is slotted on its edge into the box I am carrying. I take it out and rest it on top of the box she is carrying.

Keep an eye out. It likes to burn people, I say, and tap at the bandage on my finger for emphasis.

I pick up my box and we continue to The Place with Susan asking me why I think the baking sheet is cursed and me chuckling in answer. She opens the door for me, and we walk in. Warren is behind the counter. I was hoping it would be Michael, as I suspect Warren will say no to my request. I am the partest of part-time employees, I am leaving, and Warren and I do not communicate well.

Hi, Warren, I say.

"Hey, kids," he replies.

Warren is likely in his mid-sixties by the look of him, so I suppose calling us kids works.

I have a favor to ask, I say.

He sets down his coffee cup on the counter. "What?"

I am leaving tonight or tomorrow, and would like to store these two boxes in the attic until I can come back to get them. I likely will not be gone very long, but long enough that I cannot keep my apartment, I explain.

"Sure, that's fine," says Warren.

I turn my head toward Susan with a *did you see that* look on my face, then return to looking at Warren.

Great, I say, with mild confusion obvious in my tone.

"Just put it out of the way of the stuff we need to get to on a regular basis. There's enough room up there," he says as he walks the length of the bar and turns to walk the short hall back to the bathrooms.

Susan and I follow and by the time I catch up to him, he is already grabbing the cord on the ceiling to pull down the attic ladder.

"Move the cups and napkins to the front side and bring a box of twelve ouncers down when you're done," he adds walking back to the front of the store. There is the Warren that I know and am often confused by.

I lean against the ladder and climb up while holding the box, trying to not hit the opening as I go through so the box does not slip from my grasp. I find a space at the back and set the box down. The attic is cramped, but my boxes will not get in the way. I move a box of art from a previous show, which the artist still has not picked up, to the front of the space so that someone will see it and potentially do something about it.

Susan hands the other box up to me, then disappears into the bathroom without comment. I stack my boxes toward the back, grab a box of cups, and let them slide down the ladder hitting the floor below—they are paper cups so they can take it.

I bring the cups behind the bar, grab a box knife, slice open the top, and leave it for Warren to deal with. He seems to be on his own today, but it is not at all busy—only three people sitting each at their own tables, spread around the room.

I sit at a table on the stage and after a few minutes, Susan walks out into the main room. She joins me at the table and sets a cassette in front of me. On the label, in black ink, reads *4 Jills - Zoo Love*. I eye the tape, then her.

"It's a copy of our demo. The recording is pretty terrible, but the songs are good," she explains, and adds, "I don't have a case for it."

I pick up the tape and realize it is a going-away present. I close my eyes and try very hard to say thank you with as much sincerity as I can muster— and mostly I do not fumble it with my usual over-thinking awkwardness.

"You're welcome. Give it a listen and then write me a letter about what you think," she says as she stands and pushes her chair back in its place under at the table.

She places both her hands on the back of the chair and looks at me directly in my eyes, holding my attention. It begins to feel very awkward, but I find I cannot look away. She inhales through her nose over the course of several seconds and exhales through her mouth for about the same amount of time. She picks up the cursed baking sheet.

"At some point, you're going to have to express what's going on inside that brain of yours. Consider being intentional about it. I do not recommend the alternative. Goodbye."

She turns and walks out without looking back. I do not think it is a proper absquatulation, but leaving when she is done with something seems to be another of Susan's superpowers.

I put the cassette tape in my back pocket, unsure of how I will be able to listen to it since I do not have anything to play it with. After a few minutes, I follow Susan's lead and leave The Place with a quick wave of thanks to Warren as I go. I look to my right as I step onto the sidewalk. I can see Susan a couple of blocks away, likely walking back to her place with her brand new, used kitchenware.

I walk to 21st and turn north to walk along it. I do not have a destination in mind, but suspect my path is relatively similar to that of my first wander though this neighborhood. On and on, block by block, past *Cinema 21*, *Casa U-Betcha*, boutique store after boutique store, the hospital, houses, and as I get to the intersection with Thurman, the overwhelming stench of those overworked copiers.

I look back over my shoulder to *Afuri* and consider a quick bowl of ramen, but the small, rectangle in my other back pocket is about as thin as the tape from Susan—not enough money in my wallet for food and for leaving.

I walk up to 23rd and can see a Public coming along from the north. I wait at the stop and in moments I am taking my first ride on Portland's free public transport system. I wonder why I did not use it prior—though all the walking has definitely been good for me.

I hop off at 23rd and Glisan and head back into my apartment. It is empty save for my backpack and sleeping bag sitting next to the door. I spend a few minutes thinking about my time in the apartment and am reminded how I am glad, in a way, that I do not have to deal with finding a home for the stolen TV—though I am sure Susan would take that, too.

I look down at my sleeping bag and shake my head. No reason to stay another night. I toss the keys to the floor in the middle of the room. Sherman can figure it out.

I walk out the door, down the path, open the gate, and let it slam shut behind me. It feels like a good idea to slam doors on things that are purposefully being left behind.

I walk east, retracing my original route, to *Union Station*. Inside, I walk up to the Amtrak counter, wishing I could take the Shin, and set what is the last of my money in front of the clerk.

The furthest south this will take me, please, I say.

The clerk eyes the small stack of bills, then looks at me. He shrugs and grabs a paper slip to write out my ticket.

"Have a pleasant, short journey. You can board now if you like."

I grab the slip and note that the last of my money will not get me past the Oregon-California border. I walk through the lobby toward the doors out to the tracks. No one is sitting here waiting for a train. No one is waiting by the door's threshold to check my ticket either.

I walk along the faded-paint line that guides passengers safely to the Amtrak train and find my carriage is directly in front of me. I see no porters porting, nor conductors conducting. I walk up the steps and find no one is inside either. I have the carriage to myself. There is no one in front of me blocking my way, no one putting luggage on the racks above, no one settling in to a seat, no one looking between their ticket and seat number realizing they are in the wrong spot. Beyond the low *grumble-hum* of the train's engine, it is completely quiet.

I find my assigned seat, set my pack on the seat next to mine, and sit down to look out the window at the station and the lights of the city beyond. It is much darker than I would expect, as if a fog has settled in, except not at ground level. I can easily make out the station, but the buildings beyond are barely visible. I wonder how it took me so long to get to the train. I left the apartment at midday and it is a thirty-minute walk at most. Yet, the sun is gone and I can barely make out the full moon through the dark fog.

The train lurches clumsily forward, pulling away from the station. Within moments we are crossing the bridge that does everything—Shares, Publics, the tram, bicycles, wheelchairs, and pedestrians. The best bridge does it all. And most of the time, everyone makes it across.

On the east side of the bridge, it becomes darker still, night turning into night. I can already feel the draw toward sleep, though the jostling of the train on these old tracks slows the process. I lean my head to the side, almost touching the window. The carriage lights cannot keep out the darkness where I head.

I feel that pleasant drift begin, and know that when I wake, I will be somewhere different, without a nickel to my name.

ACKNOWLEDGMENTS

For Lands Lost

This story was created while travelling through the lands of the people of the Dena'ina Ełnena, Coast Salish, Multnomah, and the Ikirakutsum Band of the Shasta Nation.

It is clear that, indirectly, genocide made this story possible and while I wish that were not the case—and I know that I am not directly responsible—I do benefit from centuries of terror, abuse, and lies by people who look exactly like me. I don't know how to address such an inhumane outcome, but addressing it must begin with acknowledgment.

For People Met

Suzy Taylor, my teacher. She literally gave me a necessary gut-punch that flipped the switch and turned my brain on to what it was supposed to be. Literally. Oh, literally can mean figuratively now. I know, what a world!

Robert Wilkinson, my advisor and friend. He gave me his patience, time, and, most importantly, his belief. He also gave me a book that I really should give back. I love you, Bob, and I'm sorry you're not alive anymore to see how it ends.

Molly Provant for the plane ticket that got me out of Alaska.

Susan Freiermuth for making sure my French wasn't too rusty. It was.

Katie Bedford and Matt MacDougall for beta reading.

Every member of my Found Family—even the ones I don't talk with anymore. From 1985 to, let's guess, 2056, each and every one of you have helped me see in different ways. You are important. You are remembered. You are the reason I yet live.

For Her

Lastly, and mostly, Claire.

Thank you for being the one who answered the door.

ABOUT THE AUTHOR

Matthew Oliphant is a part-time superhero, swashbuckler, and adventurer-extraordinaire. When he is not talking about himself in the third person, he thinks there are very few things in the world to which a *Should* (or *Should Not*) applies.

You should help if you can.

You should work to be in a position to help.

You should make space for others.

You should take up space for yourself.

You should love.

You should accept.

You should change.

Anyone pushing a Should outside those core things is someone who seeks to have power over you—they seek to control by shoulding you into their world view. Do not give them that power.

Matthew has lived in Alaska, Oregon, Alaska, Oregon, Illinois, Massachusetts, and as of this sentence, Oregon.

Who knows where he is now or of what he is yet to dream.